A DAUGHTER'S TRUST

VICTORIAN ROMANCE

SADIE HOPE

JOIN MY NEWSLETTER

SADIE HOPE

To contact Sadie find her on Facebook

https://www.facebook.com/AuthorSadieHope/

or

**Join her newsletter for new release
announcements and special offers**
http://eepurl.com/dOVZDb

CHAPTER 1

The first memory that Mary Harper could recall was a moment of tragedy. For the rest of her life, she would look back to this first indelible mark on her mind, and remember that sorrow had been there from the start. A presence to be contended with from the earliest imprint in the matter of her mind.

The memory begins with a thirst, the house warm, the fires all lit because the doctor had been and spoken to Father and said that it was vital that Mother not be cold. Mary did not know why, was never told by her father, and only understood later that she had been spared the knowledge of how unwell her mother truly was.

Spared, but not for long.

The memory began with a thirst, and the clumsy attempt of a tiny child to get into the pantry, where the narrow window and stone floors kept the cured hams and — most importantly for Mary — the milk cool enough not to turn.

Mary's hands could just reach the key, but were too clumsy or too weak to turn the stiff mechanism of the lock. Father was out, and he had told young Mary not to bother her mother, but Mary was thirsty, she wanted — no, needed — a glass of milk. And so she began to cry.

The memory warps time, and when she was older Mary was not sure exactly how long she sat there bawling at the locked door, wanting her discomfort eased but knowing that there was no one who could ease it for her. Perhaps it was a minute or two, perhaps a full half hour, but she remembers the sudden feel of her mother's hands resting on her shoulder, and the sense of isolation lifting away from her.

Mother's hands meant safety then, and they enclosed her.

Mary cannot remember Mother's face, but she remembers the smell of bed sweat on her mother, masked by the scented oil and rosewater she wore even on days when she would not go out. Mary remembered the soft cotton of her mother's nightdress that soothed her cheek as she was swallowed up by a maternal embrace.

"What's wrong, Kitten?" her mother asked her again and again, until Mary had calmed enough to request a glass of milk.

"Of course. Milk for my Kitten."

Mother rose and turned the lock with no trouble at all, though she put a hand to her forehead and closed her eyes for a moment in a gesture that young Mary didn't understand but which she understood when she was older had been a moment of pain.

Mother stood still in the open doorway for a long while as Mary wiped the snot from her nose and eyes and looked blearily up at her mother as the grown woman stood swaying. Then Mother stepped forward and reached up into the shadowy top shelf where the milk bottles were and she slid the glass bottle out with a cheerful clink that made Mary smile and clap her hands.

The bottle slid free of Mother's hand and fell, turning over. In her memory the bottle drops so slowly that Mary can see the trail of milk that falls from its open top, breaking up into tiny white droplets. She knows this can't be real, but the memory is so clear, as is the memory of the sound of her mother falling backwards. Then hitting the floor and striking her head on the flagstone floor of the kitchen at the same moment that the bottle lands smashing into a spray of milk and glittering shards of glass.

And time is warped again, because Mary does not move from her mother's side until her father returns and a new pair of hands scoop her up. She doesn't know how long she sits there holding her mother's hand. Nor at what point she realises that the ragged breath of the woman who birthed her has stopped and her hand has grown cold. She remembers with shame the lack of understanding she had of death. That the thing that had made her cry as she sat there beside her mother's dying and dead body was that she was still thirsty and the milk had been spilled with a loud noise that scared her.

Her father scooped her up and carried her tearfully to the drawing room and fetched her a blanket and a glass of milk. The fire was built up high in this room and out the windows Mary became aware that darkness had fallen across the city outside.

Through the shut doors Mary heard the movement to and fro of men carrying her mother away and when the house had finally fallen silent and the milk was all drunk up her father returned and held her in silence for another timeless age.

When he eventually spoke, he seemed to be speaking into the fire rather than to little Mary.

"Things will have to change with your mother gone, Mary," he said.

Mary had looked up at her father and wondered what he meant by *gone* and what manner of change he might be alluding to.

"I can't leave you all alone in the house all day, and with your mother's allowance gone we will struggle to make ends meet. I am sorry, this isn't the kind of matter you need to fuss yourself over, little Kitten. The point is that I'm going to have to go away for a little while. Just long enough to arrange some things, to make a nice place for us. In the meantime I will set you up with a nice guardian, someone who will be just like a mother to you."

Mary wanted to say that she did not need someone to be *like* a mother to her. She needed her actual mother back. But she knew better than to talk back. Besides, Father seemed to be speaking as if to someone else.

When he finally looked at her, he smiled, and kissed her gently on the forehead. His eyes were wet with tears, but his voice never broke.

"I promise to see you looked after, Kitten. Even if it costs me every ounce of my strength to set you up right. I love you and you are all that I have left now."

He carried her up to her bed and tucked her in. She was tired, it was late and the street lamps were being extinguished.

CHAPTER 2

When Mary awoke the next morning, she found her things had all been packed up from her small trunk and wardrobe; her stuffed bear and the book of nursery rhymes her father would read to her from. It was all swept away into a single canvas bag which was deposited, along with her person, two houses down the street in the home of Mrs. Thorn.

Mary stood shyly behind her father, one hand holding his trousers and peering around at Mrs. Thorn. She was a severe looking woman, taller than Mary's father and with thick spectacles which she glared over whenever she took a glance in Mary's direction. But when Father had explained everything

7

to Mrs. Thorn, that severe look melted away and she leaned down smiling and said, "Hello, Mary. It is a pleasure to meet you."

Having been raised properly, Mary responded, "It is a pleasure to meet you too." Then she hid behind her father's legs wondering what was happening and where was her mother?

"Go on now, Kitten. Mrs. Thorn will look after you for a little while. Just till I get us back on our feet again. She is a kind woman and will introduce you to all her children."

Mary walked forward and took Mrs. Thorn's offered hand. Her father kissed the top of her head again and stepped down into the street.

The door shut behind her and Mary stood beside her canvas bag in the hallway of Mrs. Thorn's home.

Mary was trying to be brave, it would only be a few days after all. Father had not exactly said how long, but he had never been away for more than a week before.

"Come in and meet the children," Mrs. Thorn said leading her into a living room.

"When will Father be back?"

"Soon, Mary. Now, come and play with the children."

"How long is soon?"

"I don't know, Mary."

The living room was crowded with eight children ranging from a tiny baby staring out from the bars of a crib, to a girl who looked almost a full-grown woman. They all sat engaged in all sorts of childish play, or arguing furiously about some matter of great import in the stakes of this living room. It was a riot of noises and faces, a map of interactions she did not understand and was an outsider to.

For Mary it was too much, she found she could take none of it in. It was over the next few days that she was able to learn their names and ages and sort them out into individuals, but being a shy girl, through her fear and confusion she latched onto the first face that confronted her.

"Who are you?" the boy closest to Mary's own age asked accusatorially.

"I am Mary," she mumbled.

"What? Speak up, Scrub."

"I am Mary," she said again.

"Alright, no need to shout. Would you like to see my toy lion?"

"Okay," Mary said.

"You can see it, but it is mine. So only I get to play with it."

"Now, dear," Mrs. Thorn said. "Mary will be staying with us for a little while. So, you must treat her like a guest and share your toys."

"Fine," the boy said. "But not my lion."

"Okay," Mary said. "What's your name."

"James. My lion's name is Leo."

And James took her by the hand and led her into the riot, a small solid fact of a boy in the shifting world she found herself in.

"When will Father be back?" Mary asked when Mrs. Thorn woke her in the morning.

"I don't know, Dearest. It might be a while," Mrs. Thorn said, smiling down at her.

The oldest girl, whose name it turned out was Melanie, led Mary through the routine of the day.

"When will Father be back?" Mary asked the next morning.

"I don't know, Mary, I haven't heard from him," Mrs. Thorn said.

"When will you hear from him?"

"I don't know, Mary."

And so it went. Mary found as each hour passed some tight wad of panic would begin to well up inside her, the fear that if she did not ask the question, then Mrs. Thorn might keep the vital information from her.

"When will Father come back for me?"

She asked it a dozen times every day in a host of variations.

"Have you heard from Father, Mrs. Thorn?"

After a day or so the rhythm of it began to wear on Mrs. Thorn. She grew sharper in her responses and at least once a week would tell Mary to shut up. When this happened Mary would hold off on asking the question again for several hours, frightened to upset her benefactor. But eventually the pressure would build again, and like a mantra, she would ask again"

Is Father coming back soon?

Will Father be here tomorrow?

As the days stretched on and on...

Will Father be here next week?

Turning into weeks...

Will Father be here next month?

And then into months...

In a year?

It was the question that brought about the sudden turn, the twist that made life at the Thorn's a strange but bearable trial into a nightmare.

Mrs. Thorn was unwell, she sniffed and coughed,

and avoided Mary all day. The weather outside was miserable, thick grey fog so dense that it would soak through any clothing worn out in it. So the children were all at home.

The baby was teething and crying all day and Mrs. Thorn had disappeared upstairs leaving Melanie to keep order among the children. Order did not last long. James was pretending to sword fight one of the other boys and tipped a cup and saucer off the side table, smashing it to the floor.

Mrs. Thorn stormed in and began a tirade against James at a volume that Mary had never witnessed. The old woman was screaming fit to be tied. She had never struck her children, in all her years, she had resisted the advice of all the parents around her to not spare the rod lest she spoil her children. But today she seemed as close as she might ever be to striking James.

Mary stood up and tugged gently at Mrs. Thorn's sleeve. "Excuse me, Mrs. Thorn."

Mrs. Thorn continued her shouting at James.

"Excuse me, excuse me, excuse me..." Mary began to

repeat. The pressure in her stomach was making her feel sick. She had to ask the question.

"Shut up, Mary," Melanie snarled. "Can't you see Mother is talking."

"But I need to ask," Mary said.

"Shut up."

"But I need to ask."

"Shut. Up."

"But I *need* to ask."

Mrs. Thorn spun around and with an almighty swing of her arm she slapped Mary across the face. The pain utterly stunned the little girl, rattling her teeth and jerking her head to one side hard enough to send a sharp bolt of pain down her neck and into her shoulders.

"Will you please just wait, Mary," Mrs. Thorn screamed.

Mary stood in utter shock, her mouth emptied of any words she might have uttered.

Mrs. Thorn looked down at her astonished, and in

the long silence, when Mary was expecting an expression of shock or an apology, Mrs. Thorn just smiled.

"Good girl," she said to Mary. "Open your mouth again, and you will get more of the same."

Mary was stunned. She looked around for some sign that the other children understood how strange what had happened was, or for some fragment of sympathy. She saw nothing. The faces around her were blank except for Melanie's face which showed relief and James' that had curled into a cruel smile as of one who has suddenly found that he has a power over his enemy that neither party had suspected existed.

Things changed from that day on. At first it was just to keep her in line. When she asked the question, or wouldn't finish a meal, or played with a toy that James thought should be his alone, there was no negotiation no warnings. Mrs. Thorn or one of the children would simply hit her. It was a violent thuggish sort of rule.

Mrs. Thorn continued to say, quite honestly, that she had never raised a hand to her own children, but

Mary was plunged into a world where to speak was to risk pain. To remain silent at the wrong moment was to risk pain, and to withdraw from the presence of the others was to trigger a game of cat and mouse about the house, the final product of which would be a beating.

Mary never stopped asking the question though, even as the months turned to years. She grew taller, but though a plump child to begin with, she gained little weight until her frame was stretched over by a gaunt thinness that made her always seem sickly or tired. She was given less food, and rarely allowed to finish a meal, and since she still cost Mrs. Thorn money simply by being there, she was put to work most days darning socks or washing clothes.

At first, she was Mrs. Thorn's assistant in the matters of running the home, then she became assistant to Melanie as well, whose role as the eldest child included rearing those children younger than her.

As Mary grew older, she became coordinated enough to darn unsupervised and strong enough to carry loads of washing under her own steam. As she became old enough to tend to Mrs. Thorn's youngest children, she became no longer the assistant to the family in their various roles, but the main actor in the full gamut of household servitude.

At the age of twelve Mary was, more or less, the cook, cleaner, tailor, cobbler, chimney sweep and handmaid to the entire Thorn family, harried in her work by the threat of physical violence and verbal abuse.

Still, year after year, she would ask after her father, but it became less and less frequent and quieter and quieter until she asked the question only to herself in the quiet corners of her mind.

One day, a few days before her thirteenth birthday — an event that would be marked by one of Mrs. Thorn's few acts of kindness, a gift of a new dress to replace one of the ragged, or too small dresses in her wardrobe — Mary was cleaning the window frames at the top of the house.

When she reached up to run the cloth over the painted wood at the top of the frame, it hurt her shoulder. Three long fresh bruises were arrayed

17

across her shoulder where James had struck her with his walking stick. At the age of twelve, the boy had no need of a walking stick, but he had found it abandoned in the street and had brought it home and polished it up.

He enjoyed it in part for the way it made him feel like a grown man and in part because it gave him a tool, sanctioned by the mass-production of the Empire's industry, with which to beat Mary. Far heavier than the switches Mrs. Thorn used, the stick had left nasty marks — wide purple bruises which overlapped and covered her entire shoulder and a trio of long, thin raised welts.

She had noticed that James in particular took pleasure in finding new ways to punish her; he alone would follow her around after a punishment to watch her wince as she moved or the way she would cry out when some action agitated a wound.

There was something unpleasant in his gaze that Mary could not put out of her mind and made her afraid to be alone with him.

She plunged the cloth back into the water and then wiped away an empty cobweb in the corner. She looked out the window at the people passing in the street and then froze. A man in a shabby overcoat and reddish-brown bowler, with an absurdly shiny black ribbon about it, was buying flowers from a street seller. His face was turned most of the way away from her but there was no mistaking that slightly lopsided gait, with the left shoulder held uncomfortably from a childhood accident, it was her father. On her street. Buying flowers.

He was home.

The feeling she had was euphoric, her shoulder no longer hurt, the swelling in her fingers, the callouses all melted away. Her earliest memory was of her mother's death, and since then she had been a prisoner guarded by a family of sadists. But Father was back, he had finally done what he set out to do and they could be together.

The man paid for his flowers and turned to walk, not across the street to her front door, but down the street away from her and towards the river.

What was going on? The happiness dropped away replaced by a block of ice in the pit of her stomach, she felt sick; he was walking away.

She heard James yell at her as she pushed past him on the stairs, heard Melanie say something from the drawing room as Mary shot all the bolts back on the front door and careened down the steps and into the street. The street was thinly populated with the usual selection of street vendors and pedestrians, the narrow, poorly kept cobblestone road rarely saw much horse traffic.

Down towards the river, Mary could just make out the red-brown hat with the shiny black ribbon. He was just turning down a side street. She set off at a run to try and catch up, she couldn't lose him again after all this time. She felt breathless and weak even after her short run.

I should have eaten more this morning, she thought. The fried eggs and toast that she had cooked for the family had left her feeling sick by the time she had cooked them all and her own portion had gone largely untouched.

At the corner she paused. She had gained a little on her father and with this encouragement she followed him down the street and round two more turnings. She was only about twenty yards behind him now but her legs were beginning to shake. She felt like

Achilles and the tortoise, getting ever closer to her prey but closing the gap ever slower and slower as her strength gave out.

Her lungs were burning in her chest, a dull ache permeating her back, the bruises on her shoulder throbbed in time to the beating of her heart which was pulsing in her ears.

Her father seemed to have finished his tasks and was picking up the pace walking with a more determined stride and pulling away from her shambling walk.

She did her best to keep up.

Somewhere, a clock tower rang out midday and she hoped that perhaps he would soon be calling in some tavern to stop for lunch where she could catch up and take a rest. But the man didn't stop. He followed the river for at least a mile then turned and began hiking up the steep hill towards Cheapside.

Another aching mile or so of winding streets and finally Mary had her first good luck since she had spotted him. Her father stopped and began fishing in his pockets for something. The street was fairly clear and Mary was able to get within shouting distance of him in no time, but wanting to surprise him she kept silent and moved into the road to come up from behind him.

She needn't have bothered. Her father found what he was looking for, a large iron key and mounted the steps of a nearby house and began to unlock it.

A carriage almost knocked Mary down and she stumbled a little. By the time she had got out the way and back on track her father had vanished into the house.

He'll still be taking that ridiculous hat off, she thought smiling to herself as she approached the door and knocked. The door flew open almost immediately, and a complete stranger in a shabby overcoat and a red-brown hat with a shiny black ribbon about it glared out at her. He had a bearing very similar to her father, and was much the same height, his shoulder was clearly held in a way that suggested pain from a childhood accident, but there the resemblance ended.

"What the hell do you want?" the man snarled at her.

The expletive and the angry response made her take a full step back.

"I'm so sorry, sir. I — I got the wrong door." She felt numb, her stomach was sick. She had been so sure it was him, and now — now all her hope was crushed.

The stranger in the hat slammed the door shut in her face and she turned to retrace her steps. She froze, which way had she come, it was definitely downhill, but which of these side roads was it?

She thought she recognised one of the pubs down one of the roads and headed that way, a familiar looking street vendor was selling roasted potatoes, though when she got closer, she could see they were in fact small silvery fish that he was grilling.

Was this the same man? Had she been mistaken about the potatoes?

Now that she thought about it, she wasn't completely sure it was the right road. She took a small alley that would lead her to the side street further down the main road which would probably be the right one, but the alley jinked twice and she wasn't completely sure it came out in the right place. The street looked vaguely familiar, but seemed to be going across the hill rather than down it.

Perhaps it just evens out, she thought.

But a few more attempted corrections later and she had to admit she was completely lost.

She tried retracing her steps to get back to the road the old man lived on, he'd be able to give her directions, after all, he had just walked from her home street. But here too the streets and alleys all looked the same and spilled her out into new places that all seemed only slightly different to how she remembered. After an hour of aimless wandering she gave up. She was lost, in an unfamiliar part of town with no clear idea of how to get home. She had no money, not even a decent overcoat to keep her warm, just the wool dress and Melanie's shawl which she had seized before heading out into the streets.

Exhaustion washed over her and she sat down on the pavement and began to cry. Long heaving sobs that racked her body from head to toe. There was the clatter of a carriage coming from the end of the street and the cries of a seller further down the road. All around her were the comings and goings of people, none of whom were remotely disturbed to see a waif tearing up in the street. It was just another moment of tragedy in the vast and unmoved movement of The City.

The carriage clattered up close and stopped in front of her. For a moment she had that strange feeling she had when listening to the tale of Cinderella told to the littlest Thorns by Melanie.

A voice with the clipped upper-crust tones of an aristocrat asked, "Young lady, might I ask what ails you?"

She looked up as a face was looming out of the shadowy interior of a private carriage, four wheels and four horses and a footman in livery all spoke of quite remarkable wealth. The face was handsome, a face in its mid to late forties with a little salt and pepper in the close-cropped hair of someone old enough for wigs to have been in fashion when he was young.

The lock on the door popped and with a casual shove of his foot the man got out of the carriage and took a seat on the pavement beside Mary. He looked her up and down with the look of someone appraising a horse. "Well, child. Speak up. What is the matter then?"

Mary sniffled a little and whispered, "I have got myself lost, sir."

"Lost? Where is it you are meant to be?"

"My guardian's house."

"Your guardian, eh? How old are you then?"

"Twelve, almost thirteen."

"Good Lord, that explains your height lass, but you look a good deal younger with all that scrawn on you. Does your guardian not feed you properly?"

The man asked the question with such kindness that Mary could hardly do anything but answer honestly, crying as she spilled out the litany of abuses she had suffered at the hands of the Thorns.

"Well, there is not much good in shipping you back to that prison, my dear lass. Get yourself up into my cab and we will see what we can do about finding a placement for you on my household staff."

Inside the carriage it was a little warmer and the man had a number of blankets and furs which he piled about her first and then himself until the two of them were quite snug. The furs were magnificent and reminded Mary of the rich ladies she would see in the market sometimes, always just looking as if to spend their money in such filthy circumstances was vastly beneath them.

"So, what is your name then, young lady?" he asked kindly.

"Mary, sir. Mary Harper."

"Mary is a very pretty name. Mary, Mother to Jesus, and of course, Mary Magdalene, who served him. A very pretty name indeed, for a girl who might be quite pretty herself if she wiped those tears away and smiled a little."

Mary smiled at this compliment and asked, "Might I ask your name, sir?"

"I am Randolph, Mary. No need to stand on sirs or Misters, since we are to be friends. Randolph and Mary, the closest bosom buddies."

The carriage rattled on towards the edge of town to the areas where the houses were further back from the road, and came each with a garden enclosed by trees. The kind of place Mary had never dreamed she might one day visit. The carriage paused at a large iron gate while the coachman unlocked the large padlock and chains that held them closed.

Then the carriage proceeded up the drive towards an imposing neo-gothic structure built round with towers and gargoyles, grotesques and buttresses.

Despite its old fashioned design the building looked newly built and when Mary was bundled inside she found the place was not the draughty old castle its architecture pretended to be, but a bright, spacious and warm home with high ceilings and thick deep-pile carpeting, tapestries on the hardwood walls and ornate gaslight fixtures on every wall to light the way at night.

She felt sure it must be a dream, but when she touched the bannisters the wood was hard to the touch, as real as the clothes she was standing in.

Randolph handed her off to a kindly servant called Estella who took her to the kitchen and fed her, drew a bath for her, and took her to a small room in which a four-poster bed with sheets heated by a coal-filled bed warmer stood. Estella tucked her in and told her to sleep well, which Mary was doing within minutes of her head hitting the goose down pillows.

CHAPTER 3

*M*ary woke up in the warmest bed she had ever slept in. Her whole life she had been cold, given one blanket, sleeping in a small room with a draughty window. She was not allowed to share a bed with the Thorn children since she was seen as a servant and so she became used to a harsh chill on her skin.

Here the room was so well heated, the blankets so thick and warm, that she felt almost stifled by the heat. She threw off the blankets and revelled in the fact that she was warm, and so far as she could tell, safe from the kind of regular beating that the Thorns had handed out so frequently.

She lay there in a silk nightdress, luxuriating in the warmth.

There was a knocking at her door, a gentle feminine touch.

"Hullo, come in, please," Mary called out to whoever it was, tapping at her door.

The maid from the day before came in, Estella was her name. She carried in front of her a silver platter on which a large mound of kedgeree was piled. The smell of Indian spices filled the room, blending with the home-grown Britishness of the smoked kippers. Mary was awestruck; Mrs Thorn would crack peppercorns into a stew and would use cinnamon and sometimes even ginger in deserts. But spices like this — rich curry and cumin, coriander seed and cardamom pods — were so exotic and expensive that she had only ever smelled them on the counters of spice merchants when she would rush through the market. She had been told once that the poorest Indian farmer would eat such spices in his daily meals and Mary had always wondered at so rich a nation.

The rice was fluffy and warm, with the delicate heat

and citrusy notes of the curry and the savoury smoke of the haddock. The boiled eggs were golden and soft in the middle. It felt as rich and sumptuous as the goose down bed she was sat in.

"How are you this morning, young miss?" Estella asked.

Mary smiled and swallowed a large mouthful of breakfast. "I do not think I have ever felt quite so good. The Thorn's were... well, they were not warm, and they did not eat rice and kippers for breakfast."

Estella smiled. "Yes, dear. The master is a kind man who collects for himself all manner of waif and stray. He has nearly twenty dogs in his kennels, every single one of them saved from the streets of London. There is no man alive with a bigger heart. Why, he even pays his servants a King's ransom. I've worked for him since both I and he were about your age."

Mary felt reassured by this plump and cheerful lady in a crisp and clean maid's uniform. Like the master, she had streaks of grey in her hair that, rather than making her look old, gave her the look of being in some way a sprightly, if somewhat rotund, badger in a children's story.

Estella sat with Mary until the food was eaten down and the hot, strong tea drunk down with the rich cream. Then she helped Mary dress in a modest white frock that was a little small and of a design for a much younger girl.

"We'll get you something that fits you a bit better, my dear," Estella said. "I'll go out to the dressmakers this afternoon. This will have to do for now. You best wear stockings my dear, I can see your knees." There was a worried look on Estella's face that Mary could not quite explain.

Still, the old woman took her hand and walked her around the house, showing her the dining room, the bedrooms, the children's quarters where one day the master's young ones would sleep should he ever marry, the servants' quarters, the gardens, the conservatory, the ballroom, drawing room, dining room, smoking room, billiards room, and plenty of other rooms, far more, Mary thought, than any one man needed.

Finally, they arrived at the master's study, where Estella straightened Mary's hair and shawl and knocked gently on the door.

"Come in," came the familiar voice of Mary's rescuer from the other side and Estella opened the door, ushered Mary in and left her standing there by the fire.

She looked around. Despite the sun being up, the curtains were drawn and the fire banked. The result was that the room, with its crowded bookcases and untidy desk had the feel of a cosy evening nook. The window gave off a fireside glow too, thanks to the sunlight which did filter through the thick red curtains and the red light fell on Randolph's face in a way that gave the whole room a calming, dream-like appearance.

He got up from behind the desk and came around to a pair of chairs beside the fire.

"Come in, young lady, and take a seat."

Mary did so. He looked her up and down with a friendly smile and said, "Well, Mary Harper, you seem like a good, clean living girl. I suppose we should have a talk about what is to become of you. You said you were twelve, is that right?"

"Almost thirteen."

"And how much schooling have you had? Can you read and write?"

"Both, sir. Mrs Thorn made sure I learned to read and write so I could assist her with balancing the household budget."

"Please, my name is Lord Randolph Stockton. Sir, is for servants. M 'lord for shopkeepers. Mr Stockton, for business associates. And Randolph for my friends. You are to call me, Randolph."

"Sorry... Randolph."

"So you know a fair bit then. Addition, subtraction, and accounting to go with your words and letters. That is a good start. An education is key to success in life. I will make sure to provide a tutor of a suitable degree, but I can take a few lessons myself. My own mathematics is deplorable but I speak plenty of languages and a little French and Latin are vital accomplishments for a young lady."

"So am I to stay with you, Randolph?"

"Why of course. Providing of course that this is your own desire. The Thorns sound like fine people for a certain sort of situation, but they do not seem like *your* sort of people."

"They were less kind than they could have been."

"That, at least, is one of my finest qualities. I am as generous as they come. If you choose to stay, we will feed you up, get you measured for some more age appropriate clothes, get your education all caught up, and down the line perhaps look at finding you a place of employment within my staff."

"Thank you, sir — I mean... Randolph." Mary felt confused, still waiting for some dark purpose to be revealed. Could there really be kind people in this world, and if so, what did that say about the Thorns? Did they hurt Mary the way they did because she was not worth the kindness?

She felt a tear well up in her eye, but held back any sobs.

"You are welcome, Mary." He paused for a moment and seemed to see her tears. His face softened, and he left his chair, and knelt at her feet. "There, there," he enveloped her in a hug. The first hug she had experienced since her father had left her with the Thorns.

She burst into tears, her eyes, nose and mouth soaking poor Mr Stockton's shoulder. But he did not seem to mind. Instead, he held Mary kindly until she had exhausted herself crying and crying and crying. When she was done, she felt exhausted, as if not only her emotions but every ounce of fuel had been wrung out of her. She fell back into the chair and Randolph kindly fetched her a blanket and a cup of tea and let her sleep quietly by the fire.

When she woke, they spoke again, for hours. He asked her questions about her past and she told him the details of her father's original disappearance. He promised to help her find her father and to keep her safe until he could give her back to him.

Twice more she burst into tears, twice more he held her and soothed her. Talking in a calming voice, rubbing her back, stroking her hair, and tutting softly to her. She had never experienced such kindness, nor felt as if she had been treated more like a grown up by a grown up.

Eventually, he took her by the hand and led her down to the dining room where they feasted together.

When Estella eventually tucked her into bed, with that strange expression of sadness on her face, Mary told her it had been the nicest day she could remember.

And she really, truly, was not lying.

ary's life seemed to have started anew. Before Randolph took her in, she could not remember a day when she had been truly happy, or warm, or comfortable, or felt safe. Now she felt all these things and more every day.

The second morning, Estella measured her up for dresses as she had meant to before the long chat with Randolph. She was shown the grounds more thoroughly and taken to market to get her bearings. A few days later the dresses arrived and Randolph came by her bedroom to see her try all of them on and show him how they looked. Along with the dresses came shoes, boots, bonnets, hats, stockings, petticoats, corsets, ribbons and pins for her hair, gloves in lace and silk, nightdresses and a warm robe for wearing in the evening with slippers and a silk cap. In short, everything a young lady needed to be at the height of fashion.

These gifts were delivered over the next few days and brought to her by Randolph himself, who took great pleasure in her enjoyment, and liked to see her try everything on.

Then came the other gifts. He had a new piano delivered and an old spinster hired twice a week to give Mary lessons; he bought her books, and even toys, many of which seemed for a much younger child, dolls and a rocking horse and the like. But she smiled and thanked him and rode the horse side-saddle for him.

She must have pretended to be delighted with great conviction because from then on, he began to take her riding with him, helping her into the saddle and allowing her to choose and name her own pony.

It was a whirlwind of joy, she was granted so much that she dare not ask for anything more, but still he would come to her room at least twice a week and say something like, "I saw this, and thought of my little Mary," or "I hope you do not mind, but I picked this up at market for you," and he would present her with some small jewel or gewgaw, or some new dress that he would insist she wore to dinner that night.

He appeared to worry about her well being constantly. It made her slowly grow to feel safe, knowing that he was out there, protecting her from the many dark forces that she understood moved through the world. Even women who could be as kind as Mrs Thorn could be, could be as cruel as Mrs Thorn could be.

She asked Estella one day about how she had come into Mr Stockton's service, and Estella's face took on a beatific look that made her look at least ten years younger.

"Well, Miss Mary. My mother worked for old Mr Stockton, Randolph's father. He was a nasty piece of work. My mother would keep me out of the house and out of his way as much as possible. But when I turned about your age, maybe a little older, it was decided I must go to work and so I was brought in to help my mother on old Stockton's household staff.

"Being somewhat younger than much of the staff, I

was given the job of looking after Randolph's needs. He had a page boy who dressed him and was a kind of companion to him, but I was set to do the more menial tasks, cleaning, fetching food and water, ensuring his wardrobe was clean and his rooms tidy.

"He took a shine to me after a while. We used to talk as I worked, he was fascinated in how us working class types live, our houses, our jobs. More than once he dressed up like some common profession and went out boot blacking or chimney sweeping. The kind of eccentricity that we indulge when it is the blue-bloods doing it.

"I think he believes he understands what it is to be poor because of that. But of course, you know that you cannot understand it, if you don't live it."

Mary nodded at this, thinking of that feeling she had every morning, that there was no hope of improvement from one day to the next and no way out. The feeling of being trapped. She still felt sometimes that it would be impossible to leave Lord Stockton's house, but only because she understood how fearful and hopeless life was outside these walls.

Estella acknowledged, Mary's nod. "Of course, you

understand. So I've been working for the oddball fella, helping him with his waifs and strays and charity projects and strange scientific fads. I've helped him with all this for more or less my whole professional life. His demands are often strange, and I will not say my conscience is always clear, but he does what he does from kindness even if it ain't always right by Christian standards. And he pays well enough for me to keep my mother in her old age without her having to work. I save up in a little purse I keep, and every month I can send that silver to my old ma for her to live on and keep her two sisters. So there's that."

She said all this with a kind of defiant pride as if justifying the fact that she had remained loyal to this man was something she expected Mary to be angry with her for or to judge her.

Something seemed odd in her attitude and she wondered if Estella was being completely straight with her. But what she was hiding was not clear.

I t was a few weeks after this conversation that she began to understand perhaps what it was that Estella had seemed uncomfortable about. The secret that she sometimes seemed on the verge of blurting out but never did, and which gave her that far off and sad look whenever she forgot that someone might be keeping an eye on her.

Randolph had bought her a new dress that day, a bright scarlet dress with white lace about the neck and matching lace gloves and silk stockings. He asked her to wear the ensemble to dinner as he often did, taking great pleasure in her joy at having something new and beautiful to wear.

After dinner, he asked her up to his study to read together as they often did. Sat in the cosy warmth, she curled up and turned the pages of a book he'd bought her. It was when the clock struck nine that he put his book aside and asked. "What is it you're reading there, Mary?"

"Ivanhoe," she replied. The book was an exciting tale of knights and battles.

"Ah, yes, I read it in my youth," Randolph said. "Why don't you come here and read to me from it."

He patted his knee in a fatherly way, that reminded her a little of how Melanie would beckon the smaller children to sit on her knee at story time.

She got up and sat down. He put his arms around her and pulled her close in a warm embrace. She felt safe and loved, and opened the book.

She read a little while from the adventurous tales, soothed by the gentle stroking of his hand on her back, but after a few minutes he seemed to get restless. She read on, turning page after page, trying to get the voices right, to really draw him into the story.

Suddenly, Randolph took the book from her and laid it down. He pulled her head against his chest and held her close. She could hear his heart beating in his chest. With a father's tenderness he kissed the top of her head.

"You are such a sweet girl, Mary," he said, his voice choked with some emotion.

"Thank you, Randolph. You are very sweet yourself." She nestled in a little closer, wanting to be comforting to the man who had been so kind.

"You do like it here? You like the presents I buy for you?"

"Yes."

"Lovely, I want you to be happy here."

"I am."

"And healthy. You seem much healthier than when you arrived. You've put on weight, you have colour in your cheeks again, you are really quite a beautiful young woman now."

"Thank you, Randolph. You have been so kind to me, taking me in, and giving me things, looking for my father, but the thing I value most is..." She didn't quite know how to express her feelings, there was so much gratitude, a release from fear, it was like... "I feel like I have a father again. Does that make sense?"

"Of course, child. Though I am not your father. I prefer you to think of me as your... friend is hardly a strong enough word, but it will do for now."

"I am very grateful to you, Randolph."

"Well, Mary. There are many ways of showing gratitude. If you wanted to show me how grateful you are there would be nothing wrong with that." He kissed the top of her head gently and she pulled her head away to look at his face. There was a questioning eagerness in his face that seemed almost feverish.

One of his hands moved to her face, gently stroking her cheek, the other came to rest on her knee. Something in her stomach shifted, a creeping discomfort moving outward to her throat and making her swallow nervously. She wanted to be sick, but didn't understand why.

His hand began to pull her dress up in small movements, each one seemed almost a question, asking if she would stop him. She wanted to say no, but he had been so good to her, and she didn't really know what it was he was doing.

With a flourish he lifted her skirts into her lap and reached down running his hand over her stockings and up her thighs. She shifted away from him, but his other hand grabbed her back.

"This would be a very nice way to thank me," he said, his hand continuing up her leg.

"Please," she whispered. "Please don't."

"I have asked nothing of you so far, Mary. But now I am asking you for this."

She still did not fully understand what he wanted, but she felt a deep shame and desire to cover herself back up and run. But how could she deny him when he had done so much for her. She closed her eyes and in total silence, let his hand continue its wandering, a single hot tear rolling like a scorching brand of shame down her cheek.

CHAPTER 5

From that first night on his knee, Randolph gave Mary no more than three evenings a week to herself. Sometimes, he would come to her bedchamber, opening the door and sliding beneath the sheets with her, while other days he would simply call her to his office, or his own bed. Sometimes, he would bathe her, or have her bathe him.

Wherever she was, within the house, the stables, the conservatory, even on one occasion out in the gardens, she was at risk of him finding her and taking the payment for his kindness. She tried not to show how much she feared him, how much it hurt her body and soul when he treated her like this.

Whenever she felt the hot breath of his kisses on her neck, or the roving of his hands over her bodice or beneath her petticoats she remembered the violence and hatred of the Thorns, and tried to remember that Randolph did what he did from a place of love. Still, she felt the violence, even in the moments when she was thankful for the warmth of a fire and the luxurious nature of her clothes. In those moments she still felt the sickness in her stomach and the shaking of her hands caused by the fear of what might happen any moment, and what new shameful act she might have to perform for him, or to him.

He continued to buy her gifts, though more and more they were things to wear, rather than books or toys. She longed for the day he might find her father, or find her the job he had promised. Anything that might take her away from the house where day after day fear and shame hung over her.

Mary hoped no one knew what she was doing with Randolph. She understood that she would be seen as a ruined woman, scorned by society. So she did her best not to let her sadness show in front of the staff. Though bit by bit she began to guess that Estella knew.

The first night Randolph had touched her, Mary had awoken to a patch of blood on her sheets. In the morning, when Estella bundled up the sheets for washing, she said quietly to herself, so quiet Mary was sure the plump servant did not mean for Mary to hear: "It has started then."

Mary assumed that Estella thought it was her first period, not a sign of injury, but the woman's look seemed sorrowful and guilt-ridden from that day on. She went out of her way to be kind to Mary, but never spoke a word or offered help.

So the years had passed.

"Your birthday soon, my love," Randolph said to her one day over the dinner he had brought her in bed.

"Yes," Mary said. She said as little as possible nowadays, only when he seemed to be searching for reassurances of her gratitude would she put on a bold face and wax lyrical about some new gift he had bought her.

"Sixteen. Sweet sixteen, what a lovely age." He reached out a hand and stroked her chin, gazing lovingly at her. "You are becoming a woman."

"Thank you," Mary said.

"And as such," Randolph said, getting down from the bed to his knees and taking her hand in his. "I would like to make an honest woman of you."

The fear felt like a bucket of ice water poured slowly over her skin. She could not move as he continued.

"I wish to marry you, to make you mine forever. We shall live here so happily and in time fill all the little rooms with children."

The words *mine forever* echoed through Mary's head as the panic swelled within her chest pushing all the air out of her lungs. The room seemed very far away — the room in which she might be trapped forever. The silence hung between them for a long time.

"Say yes," he said pleadingly. "You will make me the happiest man alive. You want me to be happy, don't you? After all I've done to keep you these last three years?"

She looked him in the eye, her face a blank slate, but her stomach roiling, she was sure she was going to be sick.

"Say yes," his voice was firmer now, more commanding, a hint of threat in it.

"Of course," she said in a flat voice.

"Wonderful," he cried and leaned in to kiss her. He began to undress and with the cold of fear numbing her entire body she lay back and tried to sink into the bed, her mind wandering far away while Randolph made use of her body.

When he was done, they lay together in Mary's bed for a while, she, listening to his breathing until it settled into the steady rhythms of sleep and cautiously, she slipped out from under the sheets leaving him sleeping there.

She took her two most practical dresses, some sturdy boots, and sufficient underwear and headgear to live with. She also grabbed some of the more portable bits of jewellery he had bought her. People would assume it was stolen but in the rougher parts of London that would not prevent a pawnbroker making the sale, they would just, most likely charge a little extra interest on the loan or cut the value somewhat.

With a canvas bag packed she slipped from the room and headed downstairs. Every floorboard seemed to creak beneath her step, and every door appeared to have never had its hinges greased for they squeaked and squealed fit to raise the dead. At least that was how it felt to Mary's terrified mind.

If she could make it to the front door, she would be fine, she could lose herself in the myriad streets of London, but until she reached that door she was at risk.

Every few steps she turned her head, expecting to see Randolph chasing her silently in the shadowy corridors. She rounded a corner and froze.

There was Estella. The old woman was in her nightdress, her hair deranged by her pillow. She stood swaying strangely in the corridor with her eyes open. Mary stared back for a moment before it became clear that the woman could not see her.

Mary crept forward a little, Estella was murmuring something over and over to herself.

Mary had heard of sleep-walking, read plenty about it in the gothic romances Randolph had given her to read. In those books sleep-walkers often enacted dream walks in which their guilt was betrayed. But Estella just seemed to be wandering in a clumsy, shambling gait around the corridors of the house, her staring eyes seeing nothing even as she fixed them on Mary.

Well now, thought Mary to herself. This is a challenge.

The corridor was long and narrow, and at the far end was the staircase down to the servant's exit. Mary sidled forward, careful as she could to not make a noise that might wake the sleep-walking woman. It was strange to get so close to the woman, her eyes open, and not be registered, not be seen.

To get past her Mary had to squeeze between the woman and the wall. The tapestries which bedecked the wall muffled some of the sounds of her footsteps, which she was grateful for. She held her breath as she attempted the transit through the narrow gap careful not to touch either the nightdress or the tapestry.

She got past and breathed a sigh of relief and adjusted the bag on her back. There was a tearing sound. The tapestry had caught on one of the bag's buckles.

Mary froze, perhaps the woman hadn't heard it.

Then Estella spun around and let out a gasp of fear.

"Oh, Mary. Where am I? You scared the life out of me." She paused for a moment and stared at the bag, looked around the dark corridor and realised the hour. "Are you running away from us?"

She stepped forwards; Mary stepped backwards.

"I'm so glad, Mary."

Mary was confused, she was glad Mary was leaving. Her prison guard was smiling at the open gate.

"You should go but if you do, take some money with you. I know he keeps that from you, so you will find it harder to leave, but I have my savings for my mother, and I can spare a little silver from that."

It all started to make sense to Mary, the sad looks from Estella, the flashes of guilt. Estella knew everything, that was why Randolph paid her so well, for her silence and for her loyalty.

It must be hard to make the decision, Mary thought, between one's conscience and one's family.

Estella disappeared into her room and came back with a warm outdoor coat. It was a little worn at the elbows but otherwise sound.

"The silver's in the pocket," Estella said. "Randolph will come looking for you. You're his favourite. Of all the girls he's been warden to, you stayed the longest. He had plans for you, marriage, children." Estella shivered in horror. "The other's left when he first made his advances, or after a few weeks, when he got really... rough. I have prayed night after night to wake and find that you had finally made a run for it."

Mary felt horrified. There had been others, stronger than her, less willing to give their tormentor what he wanted.

"You look sad, child, this should be a good day."

"What— what does it say about me?" Mary asked. "That I would stay so long. Let him... for so long."

"You had a different kind of strength, Mary. They

broke, you bent. You are a survivor, and you did what you needed to in order to survive. Now you know you can make it out there. You're sixteen soon. You have a chance now that you did not back then. You can make it in the world. It won't be easy, but the silver in that coat will get you started. There's plenty of work tending bars about town. You will make it work, because you have got that in you."

Mary nodded and let Estella take her hand and lead her down the stairs to the servants' exit. On the street she turned one more time and Estella, tears in her eyes said, "Sorry, Mary. Sorry for looking away."

Then, without another word, Mary walked off into the night.

CHAPTER 6

*A*s she got away from the rich gardened houses of Stockton's neighbourhood and returned to the city proper the gas lamps were less well attended on the streets and the patches of dark, lit only by the dim crescent moon, seemed wider and wider. In fact, the lamps seemed to have been spaced out just the right width to regularly ruin Mary's night vision so that the next puddle or missing cobblestone could more easily catch her unawares.

Eventually she felt she had got far enough from Stockton to begin looking for a place to overnight. By her estimate it must be almost midnight and it would do to find an inn and secure a room before they began to close.

She found a place a couple of streets later, the warm light of oil lamps and a roaring grate issued from the tavern's windows along with the sound of drunken carousing. The stable next door had a range of carts and cabs, even a fancy looking private carriage. That was reassuring that this was both a place with rooms for the night, and a certain class of clientele.

That clientele was out in force tonight. When she entered the pub, she was immediately struck by the warm blast of air from a room crammed full of people at benches and tables, bar stools and some comfortable leather chairs arranged about the fire. The room stank of human sweat and spilled beer, of the wet sawdust that covered the floor and thick black smoke of whale oil coming from the lamps.

A tough looking man whose tattoos suggested a nautical profession slipped his hand around her waist and asked, "How much for the night, love?"

She wriggled free and gave the man a haughty look. His face was so scarred and weather-beaten so she couldn't tell if he had lived for a rough and tumble thirty years or a robustly healthy sixty.

"More than you can afford," she assured him.

She struggled on through the crowd and got to the bar where she was able to negotiate a room for the night and when she got upstairs, she found the room small but comfortable. The ceiling was low and the bed only just wide enough for her, but it had been made with plenty of straw and some thick blankets so she lay down on it in her clothes and looked up at the ceiling.

The lamp was giving off black smoke which left sooty streaks on the hook in the ceiling from which it hung. A moth was flapping about it, drawn repeatedly to the light, and repeatedly driven away by the heat.

She paused and took in her options. She could probably go back to the Thorns, they seemed to relish punishing her so much that they might be pleased to have their punching bag back, and with a little silver to sweeten the deal.

She checked her pockets and laid out her resources. There were two sets of clean clothes, a third set on her back. Apart from that she had nothing but a small stack of silver coins, which if she were to stay in inns and eat frugally would last her maybe five more days.

That could be made to last longer if she could pawn the jewellery, but it was key that she find some source of income. Her mind went back to the sailor in the bar below. It had been worth a great deal in gifts to Randolph Stockton, the man in the bar would be no worse, and would be considerably more profitable.

She felt sick. She had run away from Stockton to save herself from this kind of humiliation at the hands of men. Though this time, she reflected, she would be paid up front for the act, and it would be her choice. Not something thrust upon her, but something she chose to do.

She laid her coat by the bed, and undid the front of her dress to create some décolletage.

What else could she do? Wait five days for the cash to run out? Then it would no longer be her choice. Hunting for her father in that time would be a lost cause. In fact, hunting for him at all seemed an unlikely course to bear any fruit and Randolph would have people scouring the streets by morning, tomorrow afternoon at the latest if he lay in.

She went downstairs and re-entered the warm,

muggy atmosphere, she saw a couple of other women clearly plying the same trade and watched them for a little while, the easy way they flirted, suggested, coaxed the men into following them up to their room.

The bar had emptied out considerably and every now and again the efforts of some particularly energetic couple could be heard coming from upstairs. Luckily for Mary, her sailor was still talking with his friends.

She approached him, he turned around and recognising her, hawked up a gobbet of phlegm and spat it on the floor.

"Still too pricey for me, slut?" he asked.

The word stung, but Mary refused to show the pain.

"My price has come down a bit, I am on sale," she named a price that would buy her a coach trip out of the city and added, "For that, you get me all night long."

He looked uncomfortable, that was clearly a high price, "Unless you really can't afford a woman like me," she said.

His friends laughed at him, and that seemed to be the encouragement he needed.

"Don't wait up, boys," he said putting a rough hand on the small of Mary's back and ushering her towards the stairs.

When they got to the room Mary slowly disrobed and slid under the covers. The sailor, looking irritable, pulled the blankets back and stared hungrily at her. He seemed irked by something.

"Not gonna help me undress?" he snarled. She got up to give him a hand. But he waved her away rudely, she lay back down and looked up. The moth was still going, spending longer on the glass of the lamp. She wondered how long before it stayed too long and burned.

Then she felt the sailor kneel on the bed between her legs and his hands reached out and touched her. She closed her eyes and lay still. He stopped.

"What the hell is wrong with you, girl. You just gonna lie there, like a dead fish?" He was shouting loud enough that she imagined they could hear him downstairs. She reddened at the thought of her private shame being made so public.

"I'm paying you hell of a lot so I expect more than a corpse, girl."

His anger seemed to be growing and Mary felt afraid. This was a mistake, she thought. He's going to kill me. "I'll put some life into you," he yelled and slapped her hard across the face.

Mary screamed.

"Shut your mouth," he yelled again and struck her again.

Mary felt blood trickle from her nose and she tried to get away but the blanket about her legs tangled her up. The sailor struck her again and she felt dizzy.

Her foot came loose from the blanket and she kicked out aiming for his dangling genitals. She felt contact and he crumpled up falling backwards and letting out the mewling cry of a child. But he was not down for long.

A moment later he was on his feet and rummaging in his discarded britches from which he pulled a marlin-spike. The short bit of sharp iron gleamed menacingly in the lamplight.

"I'm gonna ruin that pretty face," screamed the sailor

and raised the spike above his head as if to lunge at Mary. Then there was a sickening crack and the man's face went soft, his eyes half closed and look of confusion replaced the fury. Slowly, he sank to the floor with a small runnel of blood trickling from his forehead where he had been struck by the silver handle of a cane.

The man holding the cane wore a black suit in a cut that suggested a profession of lawyer or doctor perhaps. He had an attractive, youthful face with the hard expression of a man used to making decisions and accepting responsibility. He barely glanced at the unconscious sailor as he stepped over him and wrapped a blanket around Mary.

She looked at him as he examined her face. He pulled out a silk handkerchief and carefully wiped away the blood from the cuts the sailor's blows had opened up. He was firm but gentle and steered the cloth carefully around the wounds and any bruises in a way that seemed to show compassion.

"Get your clothes on, miss," he said. "I will stand watch at the door."

She packed her things and found herself ushered out

by the man to the carriage, leaving the sailor to sleep it off on the floor.

It turned out that the man's carriage was the expensive looking private carriage she had noticed at the stables next door. The whole situation reminded her of that first time Stockton had stopped and picked her up, dragging her to a fate that had taken three years for her to extricate herself from.

"So," she asked the man as the carriage pulled out of the stable. "What do you have planned for me?"

"Well, miss. That depends on what you would like me to do."

Of course it does, she thought to herself cynically.

"There is plenty of room at the inn I have rooms booked at, if you wish to spend the night. I feel somewhat indebted as if I had dealt less firmly with that ruffian you would be able to be sleeping in the room you bought and paid for tonight. As such it would salve my conscience if you would stay the night at my place, at which point my driver can see you off to anywhere in the city."

He paused looking at her and must have felt rebuffed

by her look for he continued, less hopefully. "Of course, if there is somewhere you would rather, I delivered you this evening, that too can be done."

What is the point? Mary thought. She would have to find somewhere to sleep, and it may as well be at this rich man's behest as with some low life from the docks. Perhaps she would never be free.

The carriage stopped at another inn a little way down the road and the driver began negotiations with the stable hands while the man went in to negotiate their room. Mary sat in the coach and waited, enjoying the feeling of being alone. The experience with the sailor had made her jumpy and when she thought of letting this man do what he would to her it was the same fear and disgust that she had felt when the sailor had pulled out his marlinspike and threatened to ruin her face.

She supposed she could run, but she was so tired. Why bother when whatever awaited her at the end of her running was the same as what she was running from.

When the young man came back, he brought with him, to her surprise, not one room key but two. He grabbed his bags, and then hers and loaded down, he led her into the inn and saw her to her own room in which he left her alone.

She lay down in the bed, and saw there was a similar kind of lamp hung from a hook in the ceiling as in the other inn. She stared at it for a while. There were no moths fluttering about this one, and the wick had been cut so the lamp gave off very little smoke. The straw was fresh and the blankets warm and despite her fear that the door would open and the young man would come to take payment for this room and the shelter he had provided her, she managed to drift off to sleep and remained so until morning broke through the window and woke her up.

CHAPTER 7

With dawn came hope and the return of the determination that had driven her to run from Randolph's home and undertake this strange adventure she was on. Though less than twelve hours had passed, somehow it felt as if it were days ago that she had left the house. She felt renewed, the dangers of the night before had been frightening, but she could survive as she had survived the physical abuses of the Thorns and the predatory abuses of Randolph, she could survive and escape.

It was still very early, after such a late and eventful night, so she was sure her *rescuer* would still be abed. She could grab her bag and slip out before he awoke and make her way out of town as fast as possible. This inn was still well within the distance she would expect Randolph to have his staff searching, and though they would not be looking for her in the company of a man and his manservant it would still be better to put some distance between her and her pursuers as soon as possible.

She rose and changed into one of her other dresses, wrapped the warm winter coat Estella had given her around her shoulders and pulled the canvas bag over her shoulder. The key turned quietly in a well-oiled lock and she was able to make it downstairs before she ran into anyone. The barkeep nodded to her and bid her, "Good morning, miss."

"Good morning, sir."

She was headed for the door when he called her over.

"Your, er, companion is at breakfast, miss. He asked me to ask you to join him should you come down while he was at the table."

She paused, looking longingly at the door. But somehow walking out on a sleeping person seemed easier to do than walking out on someone who was sat waiting for you over a breakfast nook. Besides, the man had been good enough not to visit her in the night, perhaps there was some further mileage to be had from staying with him for a while.

She turned and thanked the barman and made her way through the small door to the pub's snug where her benefactor was sat in an armchair by the fire eating a large plate of eggs, bacon and toast and drinking tea from a cracked china beer mug.

He stood up quickly and bowed and Mary was reminded of how tall, dark and handsome this stranger really was.

"Good morning, miss. I realised our unusual meeting last night led me to be rather ruder than I should have been. We were never properly introduced. My name is Nathaniel Corder, might I ask who the damsel is that I so gallantly rescued last night?"

"Damsel?" Mary asked, suspicious that she was being mocked. "My name is Mary... Harper."

"Lovely to meet you, Miss Harper."

"Likewise, Mr Corder."

"Please, call me Nathaniel, I demand no formality from travelling companions."

"Companions?" Mary was sure now that she was being mocked.

"Yes, you mentioned yesterday you were looking to get out of the city, and I am headed out of the city. I offer you a seat in my carriage in exchange for such light and feminine conversation as you feel up to providing me. I have been travelling a long time with the sort of fellow who can talk bar brawls and ship's knots but I haven't had a good conversation about needlepoint or the harpsichord since I left Mombasa."

"Mombasa?" Mary's heart thrilled at the name, an East African port city where Africans, Indians, Arabs and the White Man all mingled to buy the mineral riches of the Dark Continent and sell the spices and silks of the Orient. It was the frontier of Britain's economic Empire and one-eyed up by its military as a key trading port in the Indian Ocean linking the colonies in India, Egypt and the Cape of Good Hope. It was as far from Stockton and the Thorns as she could imagine and this man had come from there on some sort of business. "How exciting. What was it like?"

"Strange for a boy raised on the Kentish coast. Hardly a white face in ten on the streets, a dozen languages being spoken in every market place, a heat that can fry an egg on the pavements at midday, and the most beautiful white sand beaches with water as warm as a bath. It is both a paradise and a hell. The Arabs, Dutch and Portuguese still trade slaves through there despite the British gunboat blockades and there are sicknesses that curdle the blood. Sometimes literally. My first year there I came down with four different sorts of fever and one case of dysentery. A less lucky man would have died thrice over of the sicknesses. After that my constitution seemed to toughen up and so long as I was kept in a good supply of tonic water, I managed without contracting anymore."

"How long were you there for?" Mary could hardly keep the wonder from her voice. In all her life she had never met someone who had been any further afield than Bristol.

"I operated the East African arm of the shipping company, Maltby, Maltby & Cicero Limited of York for three and a half years. I resigned two weeks ago however in order to return to England and deal with some family matters. But that is quite enough about me. You must tell me something about yourself, or at the very least about needlepoint and the harpsichord."

"I am afraid I am a poor seamstress and am wholly ignorant of all musical matters," Mary quipped hoping to avoid any follow-up questions. She was disappointed.

"Well, perhaps you can tell me a little of your story, Miss — May I call you Mary?"

"You may, Nathaniel."

"Perfect, we shall be such friends."

The echo of Randolph in the word *friend* sent a shiver down Mary's spine.

"I'm sorry, did I say something wrong?"

"No, someone just walked over my grave is all." She tried to smile sweetly.

"So, where is it you are headed, Mary?"

"Anywhere," she said. Then, feeling reckless she

leaned in and with a wicked grin added. "I am a runaway."

Nathaniel smiled back conspiratorially and leaned in. "On the run from whom? The law, perhaps?"

"No, a marriage."

"A marriage? To whom?"

"To my guardian. He proposed last night and I felt I could neither stay in his control and refuse him, nor agree to his demand, for he demanded more than request my hand. So I packed my things and headed out the door."

"How intrepid."

"I suspect he will have his folks scouring this neighbourhood looking for me but if you are headed out of town perhaps you could furnish me with a lift at least as far as the city outskirts."

"If you..." but Nathaniel had to stop for a moment as the barkeep arrived with a plate of breakfast and a mug of tea for Mary which she gratefully dug into.

"Everything to your satisfaction, sir and madam?" the barkeep asked them.

"Perfect," Nathaniel said.

Mary mumbled an affirmative sort of sound through a mouth full of eggs and the barkeep headed back to the front of the bar.

"I had to pay a bit extra to get them to prepare the rooms after we turned up so late last night, so I hope you got my money's worth, or I suppose I should really say my father's money's worth as it is not mine yet. That is why I am here, you see."

"You are in this pub to steal your father's money?" Mary asked.

"I am in England to handle my father's estate. He passed from this world into the next a month ago and his estate has been in the lawyers' hands ever since pending my return."

"I am sorry for your loss," Mary said.

"Do not be sad for that cantankerous old brute. He was a good man and I admired him greatly, but he was not given to affection and there was little love between him and me. To hear of his passing, was like hearing one's butcher or gardener has died more than the loss of family. Sorry, you must think me terrible for speaking so about a dead man, but I assure you, he would not be saddened or upset to hear it. He called me *the young Mr Corder* from the day I was born."

"He sounds..." Mary trailed off, unsure how to respond to such a statement.

"Yes. That is precisely correct," Nathaniel said, laughing.

They spoke easily with one another until their breakfasts were gone and they rose to settle the bill with the barkeep. Nathaniel was counting out the change from his coin purse when Mary heard a noise and turned to the window to see one of Randolph's footmen dismounting from his horse just outside the inn.

"Quick," she whispered to Nathaniel. "You must hide me."

Nathaniel, with a confused look on his face pushed the coins across the counter to the barkeep and followed. Mary seized his hand and pulled him up the stairs, disappearing into the landing just as she heard the pub's front door open to admit the man who was undoubtedly here to check the registry for a lone fifteen, almost sixteen-year-old girl who had caused his master no end of stress and worry by running out into the world for no good reason they could think of...

Her heart was racing, and she prayed that the presence of Nathaniel would be enough to throw the search off. After all, they would not expect her to be travelling with company. Especially not some wealthy businessman back from abroad.

She considered hiding in her room, but if the barkeep was to betray her, that was the room to which he would be sent, so she had Nathaniel unlock his room and together they crowded into the space. She listened at the door for a long time while Nathaniel took a seat on the bed and looked at her with a questioning face and occasionally mouthed a question she could not interpret.

She waved him away and put her eye to the keyhole. There was no movement from the corridor, and after she had waited a little while there seemed little chance that they were to be bothered. Her disguise must have worked.

Now she looked around and Nathaniel whispered.

"You look terrified, Mary. Come sit down." He patted the bed beside her and she realised with a sickening feeling what it was going to cost her to travel with this man.

Very well, she thought, *let us get this over with.* She threw herself down on the bed and staring fixedly up at the ceiling, she pulled her skirts up above her knees, saying, "Do as you please, sir. I will not resist. Please, just don't hurt me."

Too late, she thought. The whole situation was degrading and stung as much as if Nathaniel had struck her himself.

Nathaniel stood up and she could hear him readying himself for his assault. After a little while though, when she did not feel his hands pawing between her legs or at her bodice she looked over and he was stood with his back to her. He seemed to be pondering something, with head cocked and one hand scratching his neck thoughtfully.

"Perhaps," he said, "you could cover yourself up, and I might explain more fully my intentions which appear to have been misconstrued."

Mary sat up, confused. She pulled her skirts down to

cover her legs again and looked over. "My modesty is once more restored, sir."

Nathaniel turned around. "As I said before, Nathaniel will be fine, Mary. I have no designs upon your body and am a little shocked that a girl like you might stoop to such a trade. You do not seem the sort to get mixed up in shenanigans of that sort."

"You do not know anything about me. That was perhaps the first night I conducted such trade openly and honestly, but I have to all intents and purposes been a whore these last three years."

He looked horrified.

"You are disgusted by me," Mary said.

"No, how could I judge you for such a thing. You are... you were but a child. I am horrified by the men who put you to such work and those who paid for such services."

"Before that sailor, I had only one customer," she said, picturing the leering look of lust on Randolph's face that first night he had asked her to show him her gratitude for his gifts. She wanted to be sick. "But he had use of me for many years."

"Your guardian." Nathaniel's face as he said this looked as if he was ready to murder someone.

"I don't want your pity, and I don't want your righteous anger. I don't want justice, or revenge, I just want to get away from him. To find legitimate work somewhere so that I do not have to feel ashamed of myself." Mary wanted to cry, to get out of here and hide away from this man, whose refusal to condemn her somehow made it harder to be in his presence.

"This I can assist you with on all points," Nathaniel said. "I can take you to Kent, far from your so-called *guardian* who sounds the worst sort of blackguard. And I can offer you employment in my home where I will need servants."

Mary did not fully believe the professed purity of this man's intentions, but the alternative would be to try and make it out of London on foot.

Better the devil you think you know, she thought.

"Thank you, Nathaniel," she said. "For your offer, and for behaving in so gentlemanly a manner."

"You are welcome to both those things," Nathaniel

said. "I am only glad I was able to save you from that sailor and give you a chance to escape your guardian."

Very well, Mary thought. I guess that I will wait and see what your plan is, Nathaniel Corder.

CHAPTER 8

The journey to Kent was a quiet one in which the dreaded event did not come to pass. The carriage rode all day with them aboard and after a change of horses at Ashford they rode into the night across the Kent downs to a town a little south of Dover where the Corder estate was situated.

The house was not so imposing as Randolph Stockton's, but it was a large country cottage with room for a large family and a full complement of servants. The caretaker-cum-gardener was a Mr Whitaker and seemed to view the house as very much his own, showing a deep resentment in having to give it up to its rightful heir.

Still, Mr Whitaker was gracious enough to bring

their bags in for them and show Mr Corder to the master bedroom and Mary to a comfortable room in the maid's quarters.

That once again she was given her own room in which to board struck her as a good sign and she allowed herself to hope that this time things would be different.

In the morning, Mary was awoken by Mrs Whitaker, the gardener's wife and evidently the old Mr Corder's head of the household staff.

"Morning, lass," Mrs Whitaker said, bustling in with an arm full of clothes held in front of her. "I understand you're the new master's, new hire. Lord knows I could use an extra pair of hands about the place. What I've got here is your uniform. Wear each one three days running then put it in the wash. Clothes washing will be one of your jobs, since I have had a hell of a time these last few months churning the washing and turning the mangle with my arthritis playing up..." and she continued almost non-stop in this friendly, gossipy manner for almost a full ten minutes before the clock struck seven and she bustled out of Mary's room talking all the way down the corridor to no one in particular about what a nightmare it would be to get breakfast on the table in time for quarter past the way the old Mr Corder had liked it.

When Mrs Whitaker's rambling had died out and Mary had taken a moment to catch her breath and rub the sleep from her eyes she got up and dressed in the black woollen dress with its white apron and cap.

In society's eyes this would be a huge come down from the heights of being the ward, or even the fiancée of Randolph Stockton, but she had never felt prouder. She was going to stand on her own two feet, earning money by working, and in thrall to no man for her safety.

Providing she really could trust Nathaniel.

I t took a few days to get the hang of her new duties, but once she had adapted to the housekeeping quirks of the Whitakers it was little trouble to her. The tasks were much the same as those when she had been in the care — though she used that word with a certain amount of bitterness — of the Thorns. There was washing of clothes and of kitchenware's, there was drying and ironing, sweeping, mopping, dusting, and when Mr Whitaker found some task that did not require so much muck or heavy lifting as to exclude it as feminine work in his old-fashioned opinion she would assist with the gardening.

On the second day, Mr Whitaker was demonstrating the way to prune the glorious rose bush which dominated the central flower bed of the garden.

"See here, this dark green like an old cucumber or wilted salad leaf? Cut the whole branch off if there's no bud on it. Start with them, that's dead wood you want to clear away as full as possible."

Mary examined the pulpy looking soft green of the twig he was pointing out and slid the blades of the secateurs around the twig and ran them down to the healthy, woody base. The blades snipped together satisfyingly and the branch fell to the soil.

"Leave the fallings there, unless they have black spots on the leaves, they'll help compost the soil," Mr Whitaker told her. "Mrs Whitaker thinks they look a mess, but she does not understand the needs of plants the way a fella who works with them in and out, day and occasional nights."

Mary laughed at the insight into their marital squabbles and pointed out another sick looking branch. "That one?" she asked.

"Aye in a moment, but there is more to pruning a rose bush than just cutting the dead parts away. A rose bush is a living critter that wants to grow as much as it can, but it is not a smart critter. You can trick it, see. We want big flowers, but the plant wants big everything; given room to grow the leaves will choke out the flowers. So you channel the life force."

"The life force?" Mary asked.

"Aye, a plant is as alive as you and I. It got breathed into by God the Father sure as Adam did and sure as that black bird over there."

He indicated a hedge from which a bird was singing. Mary could see nothing, but clearly the sound of bird song was enough to tell Mr Whitaker's ears where the bird was and what sort it was.

"What you do," Mr Whitaker continued, "is cut away as much of the plant as you can without killing it, or making it look too bare. Too few leaves and it will die, but if you cut away every branch without a bud on it, and as many of the leafy twigs as possible, suddenly that life force is spread across much less plant. Then the flowers get more of it, and they grow bigger and brighter than they would otherwise."

He showed Mary how to select which bits of the rose to cut away and when she started by herself, he watched for a little while to make sure his instruction had sunk in.

"How did you know what kind of bird was singing?" Mary asked as she checked a branch for buds and, finding none, went back almost to the trunk and clipped it away.

"I'm not mad, lass," he snarled, seeming to turn angry.

"I did not mean..." she was taken aback.

"No, of course not, lass. There's just..." he paused a moment, "...a local character, who everyone calls mad Frank. He does a big round begging from town to town from Dover to London and up North. He turns up once or twice a year telling us all that he can understand what the birds is saying to each other.

Depending on what sort of day he's having they are either pronouncing him as king of the hedgerows or gloating about kidnapping some princess from him. Round here, *talking to the birds* is a way of saying some fella's gone a bit Quixotic in the head, if you know what I mean."

She did not know what he meant, but felt from context she had the gist.

"All I can tell about what the birds is saying is this: all the types of birds have a different sort of song. But birds of one type all sound much of a muchness. That song there is a boy blackbird calling for a lady blackbird though what sort of sweet nothings or dirty somethings he is a-whispering to his loved one is out of my ken."

"What do the lady blackbirds sound like?" Mary asked.

"Not much of anything at all really. The females of most of the species do not do much singing. Singing for birds is a kind of courting, but all on the gentleman bird's side. Like wearing your best suit to a county dance. Except, the fella in this case is a magpie. Ain't nothing gentleman-like about a magpie. The ladies will then choose the best singer that will have them just as you might choose the best-dressed man with the thickest head of hair."

He doffed his hat to comically underscore his final line with the shiny baldness of his own crown. Mary laughed along but wondered at how mad this Frank really was, imputing so much to the birds when a sane man like Mr Whitaker was as happy to decide on the class ranking and manners of magpies.

This seemed somewhat unfair, Mary thought. Though she could not decide if she pitied the men who must sing and await the choices of the woman, or the women who were deprived entirely of a voice.

"Oh, what about dresses?" Mary asked.

"Birds don't wear dresses," Mr Whitaker laughed.

"No, but if singing is how the men catch the ladies' eyes, what do the female blackbirds do to stand out. I would wear a nice dress, what would I do if I were a bird?"

"Well, that is a pointed question if ever I heard one," Mr Whitaker said with a twinkle in his eye. "You got your eye on a gentleman blackbird of your own?"

"No one specific," Mary said. It had not been what she had meant but now she thought about it, she had turned down a proposal and would be sixteen in less than a month now. "But, I am almost sixteen, is that not the age at which one should start keeping a watchful eye out for a suitor with the right sort of song?"

"Aye, I guess so. Though there's no rush for a lady of your fine looks. There will be plenty of time for you to find the right lad. I am sure Mrs Whitaker could be persuaded to keep an eye out among the local lads for one that might be a good fit."

For some irritating reason Mary could not stop thinking of Nathaniel with his expensive suits and fine gentlemanly features. She put the thought aside with a sneer and snipped another branch away.

"Careful, lass. That one had a bud on it."

He was right, she noted with further irritation. She had let herself get distracted. She pushed the bud into the soil with the heel of her shoe.

"Sorry about that," she said sheepishly and took a hold of another branch, checking carefully that it was one to cut. It was and it pared away perfectly.

"I will leave you to it now," Mr Whitaker said. "I have to get some knotweed out of the vegetable garden before they take over completely and ruin the tomato vines. Give me a shout if you need some help."

And off he went down the end of the garden while Mary continued the cautious work of sculpting the path of the rose bush's *life force* so that it would flow into the flowers. As she did, she listened to the birds trying her best to pick out which ones were blackbirds and which were not.

Her mind began to wander to Nathaniel. He would be up in his study at this time of day, poring over his father's papers deciding what needed filing, what archiving, and what burning. She had taken him a pot of tea before she had come out into the garden and he would no doubt be sipping gently at that and looking out the window at the other garden at the front of the house.

There were bumblebees bumbling in and out of the flowers that made a border around the rose bush, and as she moved Mary was careful not to trample the little insects or the flowers they were raiding for pollen and honey.

Her skirts were hitched up almost to her knees to keep them from trailing in the mud and the sun felt warm on her stockinged legs.

Suddenly, she was shaken from her reverie by Nathaniel's voice. "Hullo, Mary. Enjoying the gardens?"

She was so surprised she slipped and grabbed a branch incautiously and her thumb sank down onto a rose thorn. She swore, shook her hand then turned, saying, "Mr Corder," and curtseying best she could.

She put her thumb to her mouth and sucked the wound. The blood tasted sweet on her tongue.

"I am sorry to have surprised you," Nathaniel said. He looked very concerned. "Did you cut yourself?"

"No, Mr Corder. Just caught my thumb on a thorn," she replied.

"Nathaniel, please." He held out his hand and helped her over the flower border onto the grass and carefully took her injured hand and peered at the pinprick of blood on her thumb.

"The tip of the thorn is still in there," he said. "This may hurt a tad."

With great delicacy and precise strength he pressed both of his thumbs into the soft pad of hers. His nails came together like a pair of tweezers and Mary felt a sharp pain as the needle tip of the thorn shifted under her skin, then he lifted his thumbs and the tip came with them.

He released her hand and she sucked the injury again.

"Ow," she said looking up at him with mock irritation.

"You are welcome," he said with mock facetiousness.

They were standing very close together, with a mocking smile on both their lips. Mary was looking up at him and was suddenly very aware of how the sun's heat came off the black cloth of his coat. There was a pause then he stepped back a little awkwardly and half bowing said, "Good day, Mary."

He half turned, and she realised she did not want him to leave. So she called out, "Nathaniel!"

"Yes," he said turning back to her.

"Did you not come out for something?"

"No," he said, a little awkwardly. "I just wanted to check on you. Let me know if there is anything you need."

Of course, thought Mary. He is just like Randolph Stockton was, he has designs on me.

Disgust and fear flared up in her heart, then died away as she tried to reassure herself that he had had every opportunity so far with her living under his roof and he had chosen not to molest her person in any way. Even after saving her from a man who had paid her to have his way with her, Nathaniel had bought her a separate room for the night.

She returned to the matter of the roses and to listening to the love songs of the blackbirds and tried to put such macabre thoughts as those of Randolph Stockton from her mind.

After the first few days, Mrs Whitaker found a couple of extra hires and Mary's duties became more closely confined to looking after Mr Corder's needs. She would collect his clothes in the morning, lay out clean ones and if necessary, heat the water for a bath in the huge free-standing tub of his *en suite* bathroom.

Then she would fetch him breakfast, open the curtains, wake him up and stoke the fire if it was a cold day. Once he was up, she would make the bed with one of the other maids, do any cleaning that was required. Feed the fire if need be. At meal times she would serve him food and drink and, in the evenings, she would lay out his night clothes, and fetch him anything he needed prior to his retiring to bed. She would then wait up until eleven in case he rang for something and then retire to bed herself.

This led to her being alone in a room with him a great deal, a situation that left her feeling raw and fearful. Her memories of that first time that Randolph had beckoned to her to come and sit on his lap remained ever present in her mind whenever she entered the room with a breakfast tray.

She found when she did so, she would eye the knives and forks arranged beside the plate as if they were a sword and pitchfork for her to defend herself against any further predations of powerful men.

This fear seemed to bleed into her everyday

activities, she would jump whenever anyone entered a room, and would wake in the night sure that someone had slipped into bed beside her. Almost too frightened sometimes to even reach out and check that the rest of the bed was still empty in the dark beside her.

She wished to sleep with a lamp lit, but Mrs Whitaker had not offered her a lamp and shame kept her from asking for one for her room. Instead, she had for lighting, a small candlestick and a box of smoky tallow candles.

It was almost a month in when Nathaniel asked her into his study. It was a dark evening, much like that first evening with Randolph, and he asked her to deliver some coals. This had never happened before; besides, she had seen Mrs Whitaker deliver some coal upstairs earlier in the day.

With some trepidation she slipped into the kitchen and stole a carving knife, hiding it in her apron pocket, before going out and filling a coal scuttle. She lugged the coal upstairs, feeling the weight of the iron scuttle and its contents stretching and warming muscles of her right arm. It gave her a feeling of readiness and strength in her swinging arm.

The door to the study opened and admitted her. Though much smaller and less ornately decorated than Randolph's, the mood was similar, drawn curtains — deep blue rather than deep red — a warm fire emitting a similar orange glow augmented by low lamplight.

She felt the cold hand of fear send a shiver up her back and squeeze hold of her stomach. Nathaniel stood up on her entry and bowed.

"Evening, Mary. Might I offer you a drink?" He gestured to the decanters on the table by the fire. Mary shook her head gently, unable to speak. The coal scuttle clanged on the floor as she dropped it, the handle clattering as it fell. A few round lumps of coal escaped and fell on to the carpet leaving long black streaks of black dust.

Without really knowing how it came to be in her hand Mary was watching the firelight reflect on the knife blade as she jumped forwards and pressed the sharp edge to Nathaniel's throat. She suddenly realised that despite the feeling of great noise that was issuing from within her — a primal scream almost drowned out by the Niagara of blood which seemed to be rushing in her ears — she and Nathaniel had barely made a sound.

Nathaniel's eyes were wide open and his body completely frozen staring at her face. He seemed to be trying to shrink back into his armchair, constantly eking out each fragment of an inch he could generate between his tender neck and the hard blade.

Unfortunately, each fraction of an inch was matched by a fragment of an inch advance by Mary.

He swallowed nervously and Mary felt the movement pass along the knife and into her hand. She held still for a moment, and then it dawned on her that she had jumped the gun. He had made no advances on her, she had reacted not to Nathaniel Corder in Nathaniel Corder's home, but to Randolph Stockton whose home was buried deep in her unhappy psyche.

She took the knife away from his throat and slumped back into the armchair behind her. She felt faint, the room around her seemed very far away and there was an ice-cold chill in the pit of her stomach. She felt sure she was going to be sick.

Nathaniel rose and gingerly took the knife and laid it

on the table beside him, then he picked the coal up from the carpet and replaced the empty scuttle by the fire with the full one she had brought. Then he poured two brandies and brought one to her and drained half of the other one in one long draught.

"Perhaps, Mary, you might offer me some explanation for..." He paused clearly searching for the right words. In the end he settled rather lamely on, "... all that?"

With a great effort of will, Mary brought herself back to the room.

"I'm sorry, Nathaniel. It was... I didn't mean... I..." she couldn't find the right words, was not completely sure she understood all that had happened in her own mind. With sudden clarity she found herself thinking: Is this what it feels like to go mad?

"Did I do something to frighten you?" Nathaniel asked. The look of concern on his face was so genuine it almost melted her heart completely.

He had a knife put to his throat without explanation and he is not angry, she thought. He worries that he might have done something to deserve it.

It was the first moment that she understood how much she valued kindness in others, having been starved of it for so long.

"No. This is not your fault, Nathaniel," she said, summoning up the will to tell her story, in full this time. "It is my guardian's fault."

She told the story now, glossing over nothing, explaining the pain, the shame, the fear of being forever held against her will and yet sure that it was somehow her choice, her fault. It spilled out, one thing after another, in a long line, event after event.

When she jumped back and explained that first night in Randolph's study, he looked about the room as if seeing it for the first time and took a sharp intake of breath.

He understands, she thought to herself, the cold in her gut had faded and the warmth of the fire — and the brandy — were beginning to seep through to her stomach. She continued, jumping about between the physical violence of the Thorns and the sexual exploitation of Randolph. Nathaniel seemed oddly unperturbed by the accounts of acts she saw as fearfully shameful.

When she was done there was a long silence, into which she fell, utterly exhausted.

After the silence had dragged on for what seemed like an eternity, Nathaniel finally spoke. There was no judgement in his voice, and no pity.

"What you have told me, shall remain between us. The knife, what you have done, utterly forgotten by me and to be recounted to no one. Your past does not exist except in so far as I can act to help protect you from it. You are welcome here and cared for, no one shall be allowed to harm you."

He stood up and offered her his hand.

"It is late now, Mary. You may take your brandy with you to bed. You need fear nothing. So long as you are here, you are under my protection and I exercise no power over you but that of an employer and his employee. However, should you feel afraid again, you may speak to me as you would to your closest friend in full confidence that I shall share not a word of what passes between us with another soul. I will never ask you a question regarding this matter, nor will I push you to speak of it. Your secrets are your own until you wish to share them with me. If you do, you may."

With this speech done he showed her to the door, she quietly thanked him, and slipped downstairs to her bed.

For the first time since those first few weeks at the Thorns, she slept soundly and deeply until dawn.

CHAPTER 9

The next three years were idyllic
for Mary.

The work was hard, but well within her powers to
do, and she took pride in doing it well. It helped no
end that she was working for people she valued and
who valued her. The Whitakers, knowing she was an
orphan, took it upon themselves to serve as surrogate
parents to her, with Mrs Whitaker taking her to the
tailors when she needed a new dress and helping her
with her hair.

Mrs Whitaker also undertook the task of finding a
husband for Mary, introducing her to the young men
of the nearby village, while Mr Whitaker took it
upon himself to defend her virtue by scaring such

men off with threats of hideous violence and burial beneath old Mr Corder's prize honeysuckle vines.

Every evening the servants would eat together, with Mrs Whitaker cooking for them all and Mr Whitaker carving for them, and all together they would wash the pots and plates. It felt like a home, something Mary had almost forgotten existed. When she cast her mind back, she couldn't picture it, but she recognised the feeling. There was an imprint somewhere of what family was like, something that pre-dated that first memory of struggling to find a glass of milk.

In all this time Nathaniel was good to his word. He asked her no further questions about the time before she came to the house in Kent, and he was careful to ensure that she was never put in a difficult situation. He never asked her to his study again, and had Mrs Whitaker shift her to a more sociable role on his staff where she would not have to spend time alone in a room with himself or any of his male staff.

Of all this, Mary was deeply appreciative. It was kindness. Simple, unobtrusive but thoughtful, and she was grateful to be held in a state of care in someone's thoughts.

The years passed by tranquilly, the mild weather of Kent moderated by the ocean. Warm summers gave way to damp winters, but the house was always a place of shadowy cool when the sun was up and cosy warmth when clouds blocked its warming powers.

She felt more confident, balked less at smiling at Mr Whitaker and Nathaniel, was happier to spend time with the young men Mrs Whitaker sought out for her. Though, for some reason, she felt no connection with these men, nothing that filled the strange hole that seemed to have opened up on the day she was pruning roses.

Nathaniel began to return those smiles and bit by bit the two of them grew closer.

Her eighteenth birthday passed with a quiet celebration, and a solemn summons to the master's study for the first time since the incident with the knife some three-and-a-half years prior.

It was much as she remembered it, the same warmth of light provided by the well-lit fire. This time, Nathaniel did not move to the casual seat by the fire but stayed behind his desk and offered her the seat across from him.

She took it. "You need not hide behind your desk like that, I promise I am carrying no steel except my hairpins," she said with a smile.

For the party she had put up her hair in a fancy mass of curls and was wearing her finest sky-blue dress. She felt beautiful and a little warm from the punch Mr Whitaker had mixed up that contained real pineapples shipped all the way from the Caribbean in the hold of some clipper ship and a rum that she suspected had come from rather nearer based on the foul, dockside smell of it before the fruit was added.

Nathaniel smiled.

"I am glad this invitation did not startle you. I have no intention of putting you in an uncomfortable position again, however, I wanted to make some official gesture on the occasion of your graduation from girl to womanhood."

"Thank you, sir — Nathaniel." She felt herself smiling easily and comfortably. Somehow, the similarity of this room with Randolph's no longer seemed to speak of danger to her, instead, it simply underlined the contrast between Randolph and Nathaniel.

"I also wanted to note, in a more official capacity as your employer, that you are completely your own woman now. There is no guardianship or law that can bind you to me and my house. If you wish to, you could seek employment elsewhere. I suppose I wanted, in some vague way, a sense of your plans for the future. Do I need to start advertising for a new maid?"

The concern in his voice melted her heart. Here she was, sat in his office, the place that had held so many of her fears before now, and she felt completely calm. He was concerned for her wellbeing in a way no one had ever been before. She basked there in a warmth that was not entirely due to the coal in the fire-place.

"No," she said. "No. I would like to remain here as long as there is still a position for me to fill."

Nathaniel sighed with what sounded like relief and his shoulders seemed to loosen a little.

"I am glad to hear that," he said, smiling again. "You are, of course, welcome to remain as long as you like, and are obliged to remain no longer than you please."

He rose and rather awkwardly offered her his hand in a business-like handshake. His grip was firm on her small hand, conveying a gentle strength that was both reassuring and, in some way, a little fearsome.

"About my past..." Mary said, as they both sat back down.

"No need to say anything more on the subject," he said kindly.

But there was a pressure of feeling in her chest that drove her to speak on. "I want to tell you," she said. "While I was under the guardianship of Mister Stockton — if we can still call my tenure in his household that of a ward under a guardian and not a prisoner under a bailiff — I was to all intents and purposes an orphan. My mother died when I was very small. It is, in fact, the first thing I can clearly remember about my life, the image of her death."

Mary shivered a little at the memory, the coldness of her mother's skin, the spilled milk, and the strange feeling that it was she who had killed her mother. It was a pang of guilt she could not shake no matter how carefully or fully she recounted the facts that proved her innocence. Her extreme youth seemed no excuse for whatever arcane force of childish will had pulled her mother from her bed to die on the kitchen floor.

Mary shook her head, as if the action might shake the thought away like a dog shakes off water, but the thought lingered as she continued.

"But I was orphaned by a living father. He disappeared shortly after my mother's death, leaving me in the hands of the Thorn family, who were kind for a while... then cruel for far longer. When I ended up under the care — again, if we are to use that word — of Mister Stockton he promised me he would continue to search for my father. I used to think that the search for my father was a driving force. Something that propelled me."

"You were a child, to yearn for a parent is not unusual, even longing for two would not seem greedy," Nathaniel said.

"But that is just it. It was not a force in my life, driving me on some quest. It was an anchor fixing me to the first thing that seemed to fulfil that wish of finding a father. I did not stay with Stockton because he was helping me find my father. I stayed with him because I knew, and still know, that I will never see my real father again. Stockton was the closest thing I had. At first, he filled that hole, and then he used that power to bind me to him. And because all I wanted was a father, I let him. I was pinned down by an anchor of longing."

"You were small and you were afraid. A mere child. You cannot blame yourself for not knowing all this about yourself back then."

"I only ran because I realised he was never to be a father to me, never intended it. The day I ran, he proposed marriage to me. It felt like he had asked me to sign my own execution orders and then celebrate with him about my impending death."

Nathaniel's face seemed tortured by something, and Mary worried she had gone too far, said too much, and turned him against her. Was she being too dramatic? She panicked. He had been so kind she did not want to lose him now over some poorly phrased part of her tale. He had been so accepting of her past before she had thought it was safe...

"I — I'm sorry," she said, hanging her head.

"Do not be." He seemed angry. "Do not ever be sorry for what another person did to you. That beast is to blame for every god-less thing he did to you. And I mean *to* you. You were a child, there was no part of you that could have accepted his advances even if you had known enough to understand them. He was of age, the heir to land and wealth, a man with the vote, and he tricked, bribed and bullied you. If I appear angry, it is wholly with him; if these were still the days of duellists, I dare say I would try my aim against his."

His diatribe had scared her at first, then soothed her, and finally wrapped around her in a warm protective embrace. It was the fury of a mother swan defending the nest and it made her feel good to be included under the wings of his domestic protection.

She felt that familiar glow of warmth towards him again, the one she had felt so strongly in the rose garden.

"Thank you, Nathaniel," she said with all the warmth she could muster. "I cannot tell you how that reassures me, comforts me... thank you."

He fell silent, somewhat embarrassed by his accidental venting of so much emotion before another person. It was his turn to awkwardly apologise and be reassured of her forgiveness.

There was a long pause in which Mary sought hard for the right words to continue the conversation. A long pause in which she could tell that Nathaniel too was struggling with the same knotty issue.

Eventually she spoke. "My gratitude extends far beyond your gentlemanly and kindly conduct tonight. This position, this home you have given me, it..." She failed again to find the words to say what she felt, and shook her head before she was able to try again. "When I was a girl under Stockton's wardship, I was as you say a frightened and small thing. I felt dwarfed by the powers around me as every child does. But I do not feel that anymore. I am not afraid of what is behind those doors and I am no longer looking for a father, because I have a family here, one that gives me all I would ever need or had ever wanted from the father that abandoned me. I am not that little girl, you have allowed me to grow up into a woman who is no longer afraid of her own shadow."

"You were never that afraid," he said. "When I met

you, you were setting a course through the world, making what sacrifices you needed to."

"I was terrified, but perhaps I have always had some quality of the survivor," she said and allowed herself this small compliment and nodded appreciatively to him.

"So," Nathaniel said. "Does this lack of fear mean you plan to leave us?"

"No," Mary said. "On one condition."

"What is that?"

"That tonight not be the last of our talks like this one."

Nathaniel leaned across the table and offered her his hand.

"I promise," he said.

"Then I'll stay," she said, taking his hand in hers tightly as she could.

As she held it, she felt filled with warmth and love. *I might never let go*, she thought to herself.

CHAPTER 10

*I*n some ways she never did.

It was Mrs Whitaker who saw it first, complaining that Mary was taking no interest in any of the young men she sent her way and turning them down without ever really *giving them the chance they deserve.* She complained long about this to Mr Whitaker who eschewed tobacco when the sun was up and, on the Sabbath, but liked to indulge in a pipe full of foul-smelling Turkish blend by the fireplace most evenings.

After drawing deep on his pipe and enjoying the hot-coal glow of the bowl as he did so, he replied to her that, "Perhaps the lass already has a beau in mind, eh?"

"But who could she possibly have met that we do not have the particulars of? I am most careful to chaperone her when she's out among the men of the village and I am sure if she was cavorting with someone in town the gossip would make its way back to me. You know how the ladies like to talk."

"I do, and I know how well you like to listen, my love," he said with a wink.

Mrs Whitaker grabbed a bit of loose wool, balled it up and flicked it at Mr Whitaker's ear. "You terrible man," she said, chuckling.

He plucked the fleck of wool and dropped it into the mouth of his pipe to dispose of it. "Perhaps we must look a little closer to home," he suggested. "There might be some man we have not even considered for her."

"Oh, Mr Whitaker. You are an old letch. She would never go about pining for a man like you. Even I can only love you for the qualities of your soul. Look at that belly you have grown for me. Such generosity shows in the weakness of the flesh and the beauty of the soul."

"A girl like her might fall for me. You did, after all, Mrs Whitaker, and you could beat her out for a beauty in my eyes."

This time it was a full ball of wool that hit Mr Whitaker in the side of the head.

"Be serious, you old coot," she said. "I want that girl married off soon. She has had a hard life and it will not ease up until she has a man looking after her needs and giving her babies to raise." She fell silent for a moment, realising what she had said. The two of them had never had children and in their younger years that had put a strain on their marriage. She quickly brushed over her slip up. "What do you suggest?"

"I suggest letting nature take its course. If she has found a man, I am sure he will not take long in proposing. Though we might chivvy him along a bit in that regard I suppose. The master's shotguns are rarely kept well under lock and key and I have as good an eye with one of those old flintlocks as I ever did."

"You could not hit a barn door from a yard away."

"And I stand by my statement, for I still cannot. But I am sure if we look about, we will see where her heart's desire lies and then we can suitably manipulate the situation to everyone's satisfaction. Who might she secretly harbour such feelings for, that may spend time beneath this very roof even? Just like a thief in the night."

At this the penny finally dropped and without assistance from any other source Mrs Whitaker saw clearly the situation. "Mr Nathaniel Corder!" she cried.

"You must, of course, be correct. Though how you figured it out is beyond my ken," Mr Whitaker said with a knowing smile on his face that earned him a pelting with the rest of Mrs Whitaker's balls of wool.

Mary spent many evenings after her birthday in Mr Corder's office, talking long into the night. Mary's past was no longer a subject forbidden to discuss; instead, they spoke freely with one another on every topic under the sun.

Nathaniel told her of the exotic worlds he had visited in his travels and she recounted the many strangeness's of her youth, the local gossip of the town. They laughed together at the boys who courted her, though neither ever really spoke about why such boys should be mocked. Mary hoped he laughed them down out of jealousy, while he hoped she laughed them down because they were not him.

Mrs Whitaker commented to Mary one night that she seemed to spend a great deal of time with the master and shouldn't she perhaps push him to make an honest woman of her.

Mary laughed it off lightly. "What a frightful thing to say about your employer, Mrs Whitaker. Our conversations are nothing more than that, and had between a servant and the served no less."

"Well then," Mrs Whitaker said, more convinced than ever of her theory. "I will say no more on the matter, my dear. Though in my experience a man of Mr Corder's age and fortune should be looking for a pretty young wife, and a pretty young lass like you should be looking for a man of Mr Corder's age and fortune. But I'll say no more on the matter."

She continued to say she would say no more on the matter for another three-quarters of an hour, mentioning that men do not spend time with pretty girls for their edification but for other reasons that are the most natural in the world. Though, of course, they should not be trusted nor indulged until marriage had legalised such things for the couple. Though of course she would say nothing further on the matter.

When she was quite done, Mary thanked her politely for her advice and made her way to her room, with a worrying sense that some secret she had been nursing in her breast was in fact writ large for all to see.

Who else might suspect her feelings for Nathaniel? she wondered. Nathaniel himself perhaps. She lay in bed restlessly wondering.

Meanwhile, in the upstairs study, Mrs Whitaker called on Mr Corder with the excuse of refilling the lamps which were, by Nathaniel's guess at least four-fifths full of oil already. But Mrs Whitaker was an insistent old bird and Nathaniel liked her, so she was allowed to bustle in and pretend to fill the lamps while he pretended to read and not be waiting for her to raise whatever minor complaint or request, she had.

He was therefore rather surprised when Mrs Whitaker asked him. "When are you going to ask Mary to marry you, sir?"

She paused dramatically to allow the shocked expression to drain away from his face, for which he was rather grateful.

"I understand," she continued, "your caution and you taking the time to make such a decision. But she is a beautiful girl and much too good a catch to stay un-wed for long. You will lose her to some handsome young upstart without a hint of class or a fortune to his name, but what he will beat you out on is boldness. If I am not being too bold myself, sir."

Having collected himself from the shock of being so addressed, Nathaniel responded cautiously. "Is it so obvious that I love her?"

"Only to me," Mrs Whitaker said. "Well, perhaps my husband has some inkling that there might be an affection. But on the whole, it is just myself. For now. Sir."

Nathaniel paused and looked at this strange old woman with the motherly face and wondered what to do. This was impertinence of the highest order and he would be well within his rights as her employer to exact some kind of punishment. But it was hard to muster the anger when her impertinence was so very pertinent. Instead of telling her off he softened.

"So what would you recommend, Mrs Whitaker?"

"A proposal, Mr Corder. And a — a bloody prompt one, sir. If you will pardon my French."

I t was just two days later that Nathaniel plucked up the courage to ask the question. They were sat in his study having one of their normal talks. He had picked a beautiful red rose from the garden and had it on the desk before him.

"What is the rose for?" Mary asked.

"I wanted to talk to you about something else, but I don't want to scare you or make things awkward. So, before I say anything you must promise me that if your answer is no... then we forget this whole conversation and things go on just the same... can you do that?"

Mary was wide-eyed and alert but she nodded.

"My feelings have grown for you Mary, to something more than that of an employer... Mrs Whitaker spotted it and she was right."

Mary's smile gave him encouragement and he knew it was now or never.

"The rose is a token of my love for you." He picked up the rose and passed it over. "This rose is not as perfect as you but it is the closest I can get. I love you, Mary. If you will have me, I would like to court you and when you will agree I would like to marry you. You do not need to answer now and I will understand if you say..."

"Yes," Mary said as she clutched the rose so tightly that it would have cut her if he had not removed the thorns. "Yes, I love you too, and I will marry you if you will have someone with a stain on them like me."

"The only stain is one of courage. You are the most courageous person I have ever met and to see you grow into such a strong and beautiful woman has been the most wonderful time of my life."

Nathaniel had stepped around the desk and he didn't know how but suddenly she was in his arms. Their lips met and he felt as if he was falling into the most luxurious dream, but this was all true.

Nathaniel married her two weeks after her nineteenth birthday. The service was small and held in the local church. In attendance were plenty of the young men of the village each hoping he had the strength of will to stop proceedings but each remaining silent except for the call and responses which they executed with ecclesiastical order and precision.

The old grey-hair who ran the parish church read a passage from the Bible about knowing one's place in society, and backed it up with a somewhat un-subtle sermon regarding the risks of allowing slaves to live among their masters. Then, with his own objections thoroughly made, he went about reading the marriage service from the Book of Common Prayer in a most rote and unenthused manner.

Eventually the couple said, "I do." And even as the old folks of the village anticipated dark times and sorrow for the couple, they left beaming on their honeymoon.

With the French Republic once more in the grip of wild popular uprisings, as it was wont to do every dozen years or so, the couple honeymooned in Nathaniel's hunting lodge in the highlands of Scotland. There they did not go hunting once but instead enjoyed the isolation and used the wild and windy weather as an excuse to build up the fire each day. Talking and spending their time in front of it, talking sweet nothings to one another and engaging in the acts most appropriate to newlyweds on their honeymoon.

In this regard, despite her anxieties of the experience forced on her by Mr Stockton, Mary found Nathaniel to be gentle, tender, and so sweet she could have cried.

Their return to domestic life marked a considerable change; Mr and Mrs Whitaker now found themselves no longer the mother and father superior of Mary but her employed servants, and her the head of the household. Though she assisted in hiring the new maid, she largely allowed them free rein in their running of the house reasoning to them that they had yet to burn the place down and that either way, she would far rather they burn it down than she.

A few weeks after their return, Mary found herself wondering about her old lives. Some insistent pull began to tug at her heart and she found herself, when stood near a north facing window, wondering what was going on over the horizon in the capital city where she had been born and grown up.

One day she made a decision and accosted her husband in his study.

"Darling, I have had an idea," she said to him, smiling coyly.

From his smirk and immediate interest she could tell that he was picking up on her completely false suggestion of suggestiveness. "Tell me all, Mrs Corder. I am nothing but ears for you."

"Oh, that will not do," she said, laughing softly. "I am

in dire need of at the very least your eyes to admire me by and at least one other organ…"

Nathaniel shifted forward in his chair, the fish was well and truly on the hook.

"I want to go to London this weekend," she said. "Let's go stay in a nice hotel, wander the streets and see all the great monuments. I do so miss the city. Though I have plenty of bad memories, it is also almost the only place I have memories of at all."

"For you, Mrs Corder, I'd charter a ship to Zanzibar."

So, they took a carriage north to the opulent mini-palaces of the Ritz in whose top floor rooms it was rumoured that the Prince of Wales' mistresses were housed.

Together they checked in and while their bags were taken up to their room, they went out to get dinner in the hotel's magnificent dining room. Nathaniel had duck cooked with spices from India and served with saffron infused rice, while Mary tried for the first time, cod steamed in cabbage leaves and served with fondant potatoes and cream. It was a magnificent meal, rich and aromatic and the astronomical prices charged made it taste even better.

It was a wonder to Mary that she, who had been orphaned and so near destitution as to have attempted to sell her body, was eating now with her husband from fine china with solid silver cutlery.

They went to bed and made love in the silk sheets of their room.

Dawn broke to find Nathaniel still asleep. Mary rose from the bed, careful to try and not wake Nathaniel as she did so. She donned her stays and corsets as silently as possible, drew her stockings on and slipped into a dress with as little rustling of crinoline as she could manage. Out in the streets the smog of London made for the most beautiful sunsets, rich in the dark oranges and bright yellows, with a blood red underside to the magnificent clouds overhead.

The Lamplighters were going about, dousing the street lights and she nodded with good cheer to all of them as she made her way through the streets towards her old familiar haunts.

She had to ask the way several times, and wondered

about getting a cab, but somehow her quest required that she go on, one foot in front of the other.

The sun was above the rooftops by the time she arrived at her first home. She looked up at the windows and saw there was a candle lit in her mother's old room. So she mounted the step and reached out for the knocker — and paused.

Something held her hand there, hovering above the knocker.

What would she say to whoever answered the door? "Hello, sir. How do you do? My mother died here. Might I see the spot."

She stood a little while with her hand resting on the cold black steel of the knocker before withdrawing her hand and moving up the street. The Thorns' house stood there, looking down on her.

She did not even approach the door; instead, she returned to the nearest main road and hailed a cab, going straight back to the Ritz. She did not even think about going to look at the house of Mr Stockton. What if she found him married to another young girl, someone she might have saved by calling for the constables or pushing Nathaniel into a duel...? No, that would never do. Even to save another person's life she would not endanger Nathaniel. Not to save a whole shipload of innocents.

She felt this fiercely and then felt ashamed.

Nathaniel was still asleep when she arrived back at the Ritz, turning over at the sound of her undressing and smiling at her. She felt safe again, and regretted coming all this way.

As she slipped into bed beside him, she made a decision to forget the past and instead, enjoy London as a stranger. Go shopping on Oxford Street, see the new construction of Tower Bridge and feed the pigeons beneath Nelson's column.

They breakfasted together, Mary enjoying both the crisp bacon with soft boiled eggs and the loving glances from her husband. After breakfast Nathaniel looked a little worried.

"What is it, my dear?" she asked.

"I looked into the man who was supposed to be your guardian," Nathanial said as he fiddled with his tea cup. "Randolph Stockton... I had a mind to do something but it seems that the Good Lord beat me to it."

Mary felt the breath catch in her throat and her hand almost dropped her cup.

"He is dead, my love. It seems his heart gave out just two years ago. I know you have worried about others who may suffer your fate. You can put this behind you and worry no more."

Mary wanted to jump across the table and kiss him there and then, but she knew that would not be allowed. Instead, she wiped the tears from her eyes and reached across and held his hand.

"Thank you so much, my sweet love."

After breakfast they took a stroll down one of the finest dressmakers' streets. Mary felt so alive and free and loved that everything was just wonderful. The street was wide and sparsely filled with the most beautifully dressed people Mary had ever seen. Each one wore on their backs dresses that would have hired her father in his old job for three years. Unlike most streets in London this one was well swept, almost entirely clear of the horse dung and loose waste-paper of the cities crowded thoroughfares.

Along the pavements were flower boxes that reflected back the colours of the dresses in a myriad of shades and patterns. Even the buildings seemed less soot-blackened than most city streets.

It was a restful retreat where the rich of the city could shop for the finest items.

The odd roadside tout, clad in rather less fine clothes, tried to sell what they could before the Bobbies which patrolled the street chased them off.

Mary saw one of these policemen taking his cudgel to the side of a young boy's head. She started forward to defend the boy, but Nathaniel held her back.

"He is a pick-pocket, Mrs Corder. The Metropolitan Police do not take kindly to criminals caught in the act. The boy is lucky to get off with a beating," Nathaniel said, as the copper pushed the child off down the street with blood dripping down the poor boy's forehead. "They hang pick-pockets who make it to trial."

Mary gasped in horror. The policeman walked on and nodded to the couple as he passed. Mary was furious. Nathaniel could clearly tell, and made some quiet distracting comments, drawing her attention to a beautiful dress in the window of a nearby shop.

"How magnificent you would look in such a dress, Mrs Corder," he said.

"When would I wear such a ludicrous get-up, Nathaniel?" she replied, secretly thinking she would look very fine in the vast array of shiny silk and cotton, with its many frills, layers, crimping, its large hoops and elaborate bustle.

She lingered a moment enjoying the thought of wearing such a dress to a high-society ball in town back home. How people would stare.

Suddenly, Nathaniel at her side, froze. Some movement had caught his eye in the glass. He peered a little closer and she followed the line of his gaze, adjusting the focus of her eyes to see that reflected behind her in the glass was a ragged old man pushing before him a cart.

"I say," said Nathaniel. "That's mad Frank from back home. I know he wanders about a fair bit, but I had no idea he peddled his wares this far away. He always claimed to be from London originally."

They both turned and it was Mary's turn to be surprised.

"Did you say his name was Frank?" she asked.

"Not really, it is a nickname. He claims the birds talk to him, tell him about some lost princess of his, so he was known as Mad Saint Francis until he became familiar enough to have it shortened to Mad Frank. His real name is..."

"It's Alfred," Mary said, her voice utterly awestruck.

"That's right," Nathaniel said. "Did old Whitaker tell you about him?"

"Not his name. I know that because he is my father."

For the crazy old man pushing his cart ahead of him begging a spare coin from anyone who would pause, was indeed her father, old Alfred Harper. He did not notice her and walked on down the street.

For a horrible moment the memory of seeing his look-a-like disappearing down the street all those years ago came back to her. But she was not a little girl anymore. She did not panic and run, she started walking after him, Nathaniel following behind her and trying to get some clarity on what exactly she had just said to him.

She tapped the old beggar on the shoulder and he turned. "Yes, miss? Could you spare a penny for an old fool?"

"I can do more than that," she said. "Alfred, is it? Alfred Harper?"

"Aye, that's my name, miss. Do I know you?"

"Not for a long time. I think I might be able to help with your search."

"You must know me to know about that. The birds send you?"

"No, they found me. I'm Mary."

"Oh, I should certainly remember you then," he said, smiling with obvious pleasure. "I have a daughter called Mary. A princess. I had to leave her with an old friend while I went out to earn my way. But instead of earning it, I lost it. I have been trying to beg my way back to her for, must be about fifteen years."

"Give or take," Mary said, smiling at the fact that he

still had not quite realised who she was. She gave him another moment to put the pieces together and when he did not, she blurted out, "It is me, you old fool. I am *your* Mary."

Alfred looked at her for a long time, processing what she had just said. "No, miss. We are a poor family. We don't shop on this street."

"I do," she replied.

"She married up in the world, Mr Harper," Nathaniel said. "It is a pleasure to finally meet my father-in-law."

Alfred seemed to be beginning to believe it, tears beading in the corners of his eyes.

"But how did you find me?" he asked.

"Providence," Mary said. "Divine Providence." She was not sure if she truly believed it to be divine providence that had led them to be here on this street. Especially when, for years he had passed through the very village she had been living in for the last four years. But it certainly felt as if the good luck had been earned by both of them through year after year of bad luck.

The police officer returned to them and began apologising to Mary, pointing his cudgel under Alfred's nose.

"Sorry, miss. The rabble like to come down here in the hopes the rich folks that shop here will be a little more generous with their change than the rest of us." Turning to Alfred he lifted his cudgel and said, "Scram, old man, or I will have you carted off to the poor house."

"But..." Alfred said.

"He is with me, Officer," Mary snarled, remembering all the years in which powerful people had bullied and misused her when she had had no station and no power.

"And me," Nathaniel said, taking Alfred by the hand.

Mary linked arms with him on the other side and they returned to the Ritz, much to the horror of the staff.

Once he had bathed and tried on one of Nathaniel's suits — which was rather too long in the sleeve and legs for him — he looked more like the father she remembered. Much greyer of hair, and with wrinkles carved into his face so deep they looked almost like river beds. But despite the changes time had wrought on him, he had changed much less in those fifteen years than she had. She, after all, had been but four when he left her with the Thorns.

He looked about the huge and beautiful room of the Ritz, with its golden chandelier and silk covers. "How on earth did my daughter do so well by herself? Tell me the whole story."

But Mary could not bear to tell him how his abandonment had given her over into one kind of slavery with the Thorns and another with Randolph Stockton, so instead, she said. "It is a long tale, and I will tell you the whole of it."

With a few choice redactions, she thought.

"But for now, I want to celebrate having you back in my life. There will be plenty of time to tell you everything once we are back down in Kent and have you settled in at our home."

Alfred began to tear up again. "I am to live with you?"

"Of course," Nathaniel said. "You are family."

For the first time in a long while, Mary felt that was true, without qualification or absence. They were a full family. Her missing father was here, her husband was here, and watching over all of them from Heaven, the ghostly presence of her mother.

The three of them embraced, and she finally felt complete.

THE ORPHAN'S COURAGE PREVIEW

Valeria Collins squinted as the dull, grey light filtered through the filthy window. She stifled a yawn and tried to wake to another dreary morning of cold and spitting rain. It was typical of London at this time of year.

Her first thought was surprise that Miss June, the woman who ran the orphanage, hadn't made them scrub the cracked glass, with vinegar and newspaper, for at least a week. Her second was one of cold and discomfort. The wind howled through the gaps in the window and ran over her shoulder. Trying to pull the thin, dirty blanket up, she wished that Caroline would stop kneeing her in the back.

A shiver ran through her, and she huddled under the thin blanket, inching closer to her pallet mates. Despite the fact that Caroline slept in a tight ball, at least she was warm. Lucy snuggled closer to Valeria in her sleep, snuffling in the little girl way that she had even though she was nearly eight. To one side, Nora, her best friend, looked cold and small. Her thin body shook and Valeria moved closer to her, inching the blanket over her shoulder.

Then she cuddled back down and savoured the last few minutes of rest before they were all roused from sleep. Valeria tried not to think about the day ahead of her, which would include the same never-ending drudgery that it always did. The girls would start with whatever chores Miss Jane decided to assign them for that day. Scrubbing and cleaning the house, cooking the water-thin gruel, or sweeping out the hearth were all possibilities, and she was never sure which one she dreaded the most.

Then after a bit of food, the girls would start the mending that Miss June took in so that she could earn some extra money. Valeria flexed her fingers, trying not to feel bitter about the fact that her hands always ached as did her eyes from squinting in the dim light that their paltry candles offered.

With a sigh, Valeria lifted herself off the pallet, trying not to disturb the other girls. Pulling on her tattered dress, she wondered how she would ever get adopted when she looked like a dirty waif you would find on the street. She would try to clean herself up before anyone else awoke. Sweeping her brown hair back into the ribbon she kept in her apron pocket, she decided to go outside.

Everything squeaked and creaked as she crept down the hallway to the stairs that would lead her to the kitchen. There she might be able to sneak the bucket out to the pump in the back. She knew that if Miss June caught her, she would be punished; taking the bucket to the pump was not something she was allowed to do just for herself. None of the girls were allowed to leave the building without permission. She knew that she would probably be emptying the chamber pots for the next month if she was caught. Still, she couldn't bear to go through another day so dirty and dishevelled and they only got water to wash on a Wednesday which was three days away.

As she made it to the bottom step, she heard the tell-tale clicks of low-heeled boots coming down the hallway. There was no mistaking the sound as that of Miss June.

Panic flashed through Valeria, making her heart beat so fast that it thrummed in her ears. She could not be caught. Looking around quickly, she decided to take her chances in the hall closet.

Ducking behind the door, Valeria held her breath as Miss June walked by. Only then did she realize that there was a second set of footsteps. She wondered who would be walking with Miss June this early in the morning.

"I have sent out a notice to some of our... wealthier supporters," Miss June was saying. The pair had stopped in front of the closet, so Miss June's voice echoed through the small entryway.

"What for?" Valeria recognized the voice as that of Mrs. Mulligan, the housekeeper for the wealthy widow who lived next door to the orphanage. What was she doing here this early?

Miss June sighed heavily. "We need to get some of the older orphans out of here. There have been many inquiries for placements here, so many people going to the poor house, but we do not have enough room. Not that it will stop me, but I don't think I can stand too many more brats under this roof and the older girls are more trouble. They eat more too."

"So, how many people will be coming?" Mrs. Mulligan asked.

"I'm not sure, but as many as we can get," Miss June said. "You need to try to get that employer of yours over here. The old bat would be a good benefactor. With her support, I wouldn't have to take in so much work."

Valeria tried to understand every word. The main thing that she was hearing was that she had a chance today to get adopted. It was the thing that she longed for more than anything in the world. It made her want to get cleaned up all the more. How she wished Miss June would move on. Holding her breath, she tried to imagine what it would be like to have a real home. There would be food every day and maybe even meat on a Sunday. It was a dream that put a smile on her face. This time it would be her.

After what seemed like an eternity, the two women

were on their way disappearing to another part of the building.

Valeria eased out of her hiding place, and as she stood debating whether or not now was the right time to try to get out to the pump, she heard some of the other orphans coming down the stairs. Her spirits fell. Now wasn't the right time, but she had to get cleaned up before the prospective adoptive parents came.

As Valeria headed to the kitchen area to start what she hoped would be her chores for the day—cooking was the least despicable task she could think of—she bumped right into Nora, her closest friend in the orphanage.

"Oh, Nora, sorry!" Valeria cried. "I guess I was just preoccupied."

"Is something bothering you?" Nora asked, tilting her head to one side so that her thin blond hair spilled over her shoulder.

Valeria chewed on her lower lip, and then lowering her voice, said, "I heard Miss June say that a lot of people are coming today for adoptions."

"Oh," Nora said. "That's nice."

Valeria felt the rising irritation in her chest. Nora was two years younger than she was, and sometimes in moments like this, Valeria could tell that the age gap made the younger girl slightly naive.

"I really want to get adopted," Valeria said.

Nora nodded. "I know you do, me too."

"I've been studying so hard," she said. "I found a book of poetry hidden behind the drawers in one of the attic rooms and I have been practicing my reading. And I don't know if you noticed or not, but I've been practicing my manners as well."

"You'll get adopted one day," Nora said encouragingly.

Valeria had to admire the younger girl's optimism in the face of the bleakness that surrounded them on a daily basis.

"You will too," Valeria said impulsively. She wasn't sure she believed the words, but she wanted to. "Just think what it will be like when we get out of here and have a real family."

"Warm beds and full bellies," Nora said, her eyes glazing over at the thought."

"Someone who actually cares about what happens to us." Valeria was smiling as the fantasy felt so tantalizingly close.

"No one is ever going to care what happens to you."

The snooty voice broke through the sweetness of the daydream. Valeria turned to scowl at Sophie Walsh, her arch enemy in the orphanage. Sometimes she wanted to slap the freckles off the other girl's smug face.

"Any of us could get adopted today," Nora piped up.

"I wasn't talking to you," Sophie snapped at Nora, propping her hand on her hip. She turned back to Valeria. "You are practically an old maid. You will be sent to the workhouse before any person is dumb enough to take a chance on you."

Valeria felt a panic inside, not the workhouse, she believed it was even worse than here and she wouldn't go there... ever. "I am going to get adopted," Valeria said with a ferocity that made the other girls' eyes widen slightly.

Sophie recovered quickly, the smirk returning to her face. "Please, you've never been anyone's first choice. You haven't even been anyone's second choice. You're just ugly and pathetic."

"You haven't been anyone's first choice either," Valeria retorted fighting down the sting that the other girl's words caused inside. "Or else you wouldn't be here."

"As a matter of fact, I've been plenty of people's second choice," Sophie said.

Before Valeria could say anything else, however, the tell-tale clicking of boots came back down the hall.

Miss June grabbed Valeria by the elbow and moved her to one side. She glared between the three girls.

"Stop this bickering, all of you. We'll not have any of that today," Miss June yelled as her face melted into a glower. "All three of you will scrub floors until I can see myself in them. Otherwise, you won't get your soup tonight."

As the three of them trudged silently away, Valeria vowed that she would do her chores and then clean up so that she would find the perfect people to adopt her.

Read The Orphan's Courage for 0.99 or FREE on Kindle Unlimited.

ALSO BY SADIE HOPE

Thanks for Reading

I love sharing my Victorian Romances with you and have several more waiting for my editor to approve. Join my Newsletter by clicking here to find out when my books are available.

I want to thank you so much for reading this book, if you enjoyed it please leave a review on Amazon. It makes such a difference to me and I would be so grateful.

Thank you so much.

Sadie

Previous Books:

The Beggar's Dream

The Orphan's Courage

The Orphan's Hope

VICTORIAN ROMANCE
SADIE HOPE
THE ORPHAN'S HOPE

The Mother's Secret

The Maid's Blessing

ABOUT THE AUTHOR

Sadie Hope was born in Preston, Lancashire, where she worked in a textile factory for many years. Married with two grown children, she would spend her nights writing stories about life in Victorian times. She loved to read all the books of this era and often found herself daydreaming of characters that would pop into her head.

She hopes you enjoy these stories for she has many more to share with you.

Follow Sadie on Facebook

Follow Sadie on Amazon

 facebook.com/AuthorSadieHope

Printed in Great Britain
by Amazon